Disturbing the Peace

The second Clint heard the shot, he dropped to one knee and reached for his pistol. Another shot followed the first, but that was just different enough in pitch to have come from a different gun. Soon the camp outside was filled with gunshots. The inside of the tepee wasn't in much better condition.

"They're trying to kill me!" Tolfox shouted.

That was all the braves needed to hear before they swarmed in two directions. Half of the warriors closed in around the chief and the other half ran from the tepee. A few of them stayed right where they were, however. Those were the ones who'd surrounded Clint.

"I didn't fire a shot!" Clint said as one of the braves grabbed his arms and another drew a long blade from a scabbard hanging from his hip. "You were watching me the whole damn time!"

The Indian who'd laid down the law to Clint was the one who got up close to him now. Pressing the knife against Clint's throat, he said, "If any of those soldiers did this, you will die."

THE GUNSMITH

320

STRAW MEN

J. R. ROBERTS

JOVE BOOKS, NEW YORK

THE BERKLEY PUBLISHING GROUP
Published by the Penguin Group
Penguin Group (USA) Inc.
375 Hudson Street, New York, New York 10014, USA
Penguin Group (Canada), 90 Eglinton Avenue East, Suite 700, Toronto, Ontario M4P 2Y3, Canada
(a division of Pearson Penguin Canada Inc.)
Penguin Books Ltd., 80 Strand, London WC2R 0RL, England
Penguin Group Ireland, 25 St. Stephen's Green, Dublin 2, Ireland (a division of Penguin Books Ltd.)
Penguin Group (Australia), 250 Camberwell Road, Camberwell, Victoria 3124, Australia
(a division of Pearson Australia Group Pty. Ltd.)
Penguin Books India Pvt. Ltd., 11 Community Centre, Panchsheel Park, New Delhi—110 017, India
Penguin Group (NZ), 67 Apollo Drive, Rosedale, North Shore 0632, New Zealand
(a division of Pearson New Zealand Ltd.)
Penguin Books (South Africa) (Pty.) Ltd., 24 Sturdee Avenue, Rosebank, Johannesburg 2196,
South Africa

Penguin Books Ltd., Registered Offices: 80 Strand, London WC2R 0RL, England

This is a work of fiction. Names, characters, places, and incidents either are the product of the author's imagination or are used fictitiously, and any resemblance to actual persons, living or dead, business establishments, events, or locales is entirely coincidental.

STRAW MEN

A Jove Book / published by arrangement with the author

PRINTING HISTORY
Jove edition / August 2008

Copyright © 2008 by Robert J. Randisi.
Cover illustration by Sergio Giovine.

ISBN: 978-0-515-14511-3

JOVE®
Jove Books are published by The Berkley Publishing Group,
a division of Penguin Group (USA) Inc.,
375 Hudson Street, New York, New York 10014.
JOVE is a registered trademark of Penguin Group (USA) Inc.
The "J" design is a trademark belonging to Penguin Group (USA) Inc.

PRINTED IN THE UNITED STATES OF AMERICA

10 9 8 7 6 5 4 3 2 1

ONE

The poker game had been going for close to two weeks straight. Having taken over one of the biggest tables in the back of the Jackrabbit Saloon, the game had brought more attention to the little town of Juanita than the night when Billy the Kid had used the place for a temporary refuge. Unlike that other time, the poker game could be talked about in the open and without fear of legal entanglements.

It was a bright day in Juanita and the air was warm without drifting too close to hot. But no matter how comfortable it was outside, nearly everyone in town was seeking the shade. That, after all, was where the action could be found.

The Jackrabbit Saloon was situated in the hub of the little town, so it was usually the first destination for newcomers. As such, nobody took much notice when a rider thundered up to the front of the saloon, kicking up enough dust to leave a gritty cloud in the horse's wake. The rider jumped from the saddle, flicked the reins around a hitching post, and stomped into the saloon. Even with all of this noise, the rider had yet to draw more than one or two quick glances.

"This where the Evans game is being played?" the rider asked.

The man tending the bar was a stout, balding fellow with pasty skin and a bulbous nose. "Sure is," he replied. "It'll cost you two hundred dollars to buy in."

"I don't want to buy in. I'm looking for one of the men that's supposed to be playing."

So far, the barkeep hadn't even glanced toward the front door. When he'd answered the rider's question, it was plain to hear that he'd answered it several times already and was getting tired of hearing his own voice. Now that he had another reason to take his eyes off what he was doing, he seemed grateful for the disturbance. Once he got a look at the rider, he grinned from ear to ear.

"Well now," the barkeep said as he took in the sight of the short woman dressed in buckskins. "If you're looking for someone, I'm the man to ask."

The rider stepped up to the bar and rolled her eyes at the man's response. Since she had gotten that sort of reception plenty of times in recent days, she paid no mind to the barkeep's wandering eyes. Once she got closer to the bar, those eyes were forced up toward her face anyhow.

"The man I'm looking for is Clint Adams," she said. "Is he still here?"

"He ain't about at the moment, but he should be around here before too long."

"How long is that?" a dirty man standing farther along the bar asked. He looked to be somewhere in his late forties and had a long, narrow face covered in graying stubble. His chin was pointed and his eyes were cast in a severe squint. Shoving up to put himself closer to the barkeep, he also managed to shove the rider over a few steps.

"Take it easy, George," the barkeep warned.

George's squint got even worse until it seemed like a miracle that he could see at all. "To hell with easy! Adams cheated me out of more'n three hundred dollars! Unless *you* want to pay me back, you'd best tell me where that cocksucker is!"

The rider in the buckskins gritted her teeth and knocked her shoulder against George with enough force to reclaim her original spot at the bar. Even though she was just shy of five and a half feet tall, she carried herself like someone who towered over the angry man beside her. Judging by the look on George's face, he surely hadn't expected to be pushed aside so easily.

"Watch your manners, mister," the rider growled. "I was having a conversation."

"An' you can still have it," George replied. Now that he'd had a chance to look her over, his angry squint eased up a bit. "Matter of fact, you can talk with me if you like."

The rider's buckskins covered her from neck to toe and were accented by a few layers of tattered fringe. A few strands of light brown hair hung down over her forehead and the rest was kept in place by a weathered hat or was tied behind her head. But her hair didn't seem to be what was holding George's attention. His eyes were fixed upon the curves of her breasts beneath the tanned leather. Her hips were slender, but the buckskins wrapped around them nicely.

Glaring up at George, the rider said, "You won't be able to do much talking once I break your jaw. Now, I suggest you back up a step before this gets messy."

George started to laugh at her, but stopped short when he saw the fire in the rider's eyes. Doing his best to keep his scowl in place, he stepped back and shifted his gaze to the bartender. "This is your place, and I bet you'd lose a whole lot of business if it got out this big game was crooked."

"It's not crooked," the bartender said. "Everyone's just getting bent out of shape over nothing."

"I'm not getting bent out of shape!" the rider protested.

"And three hundred dollars ain't nothin'!" George added. The moment he saw the bartender look over to the rider, George lunged over the bar to grab the man by the front of his shirt. "The bitch will wait her turn! I want this matter resolved right now!"

"What did you just call me?" the rider asked.

"You heard me, dammit. Now just wait yer turn!"

Before the bartender could say a word to either of them, he saw the rider pull back her arm and send a fist straight into George's mouth. Although George was stunned by the blow, he obviously wasn't going to take his lumps and be done with it. His hand flashed toward the gun at his hip as a string of obscenities spewed from his mouth.

So far, the men at the game in the back of the room hadn't looked away from their cards.

TWO

"Hold on, hold on!" the barkeep pleaded.

Neither George nor the rider seemed to hear a word coming from the bartender's mouth. Instead, George was fumbling for his gun while the rider took a few steps back to put some space between herself and the man she'd just punched.

George's draw wasn't quick and it wasn't pretty, but it got the job done. By the time he pulled the rusty .44 from its holster, George was muttering, "I ain't one for hurting a woman, but no bitch is gonna smack me around like that."

Lunging forward to close the distance between them, the rider said, "If you talk to all ladies like that, I'm surprised you don't get smacked around more often."

Although George had his gun in hand, he hadn't brought it up to aim it at her just yet. He shook his head and took a step back while raising his arm. He took half a step before stopping. George's eyes widened to the size of saucers and his gun hand froze a few inches shy of taking proper aim. Although the rider was still directly in front of him, George wasn't looking at her. Instead, he pulled in a slow breath and slowly shifted his eyes downward until he got a good look at what was happening below his belt.

The rider's hand was down there and it was wrapped around the handle of a hunting knife. The blade of that knife was wedged between George's legs so the sharpened steel was just making contact with him.

Grinning, the rider asked, "You ready to take back what you called me?"

At the moment, George was barely able to form a word. When he felt another hand drop heavily onto his shoulder, he nearly jumped out of his skin.

"I'd suggest you make amends, George," Clint Adams said as he stepped around while keeping his hand upon the man's shoulder. "From where I'm standing, it looks like she's got you where it counts."

George wasn't about to move a muscle. When he twitched his eyes to look over at Clint, he muttered, "God damn you, Adams. If this . . ."

Suddenly, George felt a bit more pressure as the blade pressed against his crotch.

Gulping loudly and nodding to the rider, George said, "If this *lady* didn't have that knife on me, you wouldn't be talking so loud."

Clint stepped around George and leaned over to make a show of taking in the sight in front of him. When he got a good look at the knife being held between George's legs, Clint pulled in a dramatic breath and winced. "I didn't have anything to do with this lady or where she decided to put her knife, but from my experience I'd say you probably had it coming."

"There ain't no need for this," George said as he lowered his gun and then dropped it into its holster. "See? I don't even have my gun no more. Any harm comes to me and it'll be criminal."

"It'll be a favor to clip a piece of manure like you," the rider snarled.

Clint raised an eyebrow and nodded. "I'd have to agree. What did you do to deserve this, anyway?"

"I was . . . lookin' for you, Adams," George grumbled.

"What for?" Clint asked. "Was it about that three hundred dollars?"

"Hell . . . yes, it was."

Although he'd been able to get a quick look at the rider, Clint took a few seconds to look at her again. Her buckskins were obviously well worn and contoured to her body, which told him that she was in them more often than not. He could also see enough of her curves to get a good idea of what might be under those buckskins. Her face was dirty, but became a whole lot prettier when she showed him a quick smile.

"What's your name, ma'am?" Clint asked.

The rider might have held Clint's gaze longer if she hadn't been so concerned about taking her eyes off George. "Abigail," she replied.

"I'm Clint Adams. Now that we're on friendlier terms, why don't we have a more civilized talk?"

"Fine with me. This asshole was the one who made things get nasty."

"George is just upset because he's been on a losing streak. I'm sure he's had a minute to calm down. Haven't you, George?"

"Yeah," George grunted as he forced himself to nod. "My business ain't with her anyways."

"So if Abigail puts her knife away, you won't step out of line?" Clint asked.

"She can go to hell, for all I care."

Clint stepped between Abigail and George so he could reach out with his left hand to ease her arm down. Although she resisted at first, Abigail allowed her arm to be lowered until the knife blade was no longer between George's legs. From there, she stepped back and planted her feet so she could still square her shoulders to both men.

"There now," Clint said as he put himself directly in front of George. "Your business is with me, so let's hear it."

"You know what I'm gonna say," George snapped. "You cheated me outta three hundred dollars and I want it back."

"You bet two hundred dollars on a pair of sixes," Clint replied. "I just raised you. There's no law against that."

"There's a law against cheatin'. How the hell did you know what I was holdin'?"

"Because you're a terrible cardplayer," Clint replied without taking so much as a second to think it over. "Considering how many gamblers have come to town for this game, I'd think you were lucky to get out after losing only three hundred. Take your losses like anyone else and don't make it any worse on yourself."

George shook his head slowly and then faster until he seemed close to twisting it clean off his shoulders. "Oh, no. To hell with this and to hell with the both of you! First this bitch here thinks she can push me around and then you wanna keep what you took from me?"

"Don't push it, George," Clint said in a steady tone. "I'm warning you."

By now, several men from the game in the back of the room as well as the rest of the patrons in the saloon were watching what was happening at the bar. Some of the faces were amused by George's predicament, while several seemed to be more concerned with what would happen to Clint.

"You gonna hand back my three hundred?" George asked.

"No," Clint said. "But I'll give you a chance to win it back in a game between you and me. No buy-in necessary. How's that?"

"How's that? I'll tell you how's that! If there's gonna be a game between you and me, this is the only game I want!" With that, George clamped his hand around his gun and pulled it once more from its holster. He moved quicker this time and his eyes were set upon his target, but he still wasn't fast enough.

Clint snapped his hand down and drew his own modified Colt from the holster at his side in a flicker of motion. He cleared leather before George could even touch his trigger. "You already made enough bad moves today, George," Clint warned. "Don't make this one your last."

Although George wasn't moving, every muscle in his body twitched anxiously. His teeth ground together. His lips turned white as they drew into a pair of tight lines. His fingers tightened around the grip of his .44 and his chest strained with his next breath.

Sensing the dilemma within the man, Clint narrowed his eyes and cocked his head to one side in a simple gesture that said more than enough. The moment George took his eyes off him to glance at the rest of the men in the saloon, Clint knew the fight was over.

"Keep yer damn money," George grunted. "You'll probably just cheat me again anyways."

"You sure about that, George?" Clint asked.

Picking up on the meaning of Clint's question, George shook his head and eased his gun back into its holster. "Or . . . maybe you didn't cheat. It was only a pair of goddamned sixes."

Clint nodded. "Happens to the best of us."

"You'd best be leaving, George," the bartender said. "Sleep off that whiskey."

The saloon was quiet for a few more seconds until George finally let out his breath and took his hand away from his holster. As if picking up on George's defeat, the players got back to their games and the locals got back to their drinks. If George had a tail, he would have tucked it between his legs as he scurried out of the saloon.

When Clint looked back at Abigail, he tipped his hat and said, "Hope you don't mind me stepping in like that. Things looked like they were about to get messy."

"They were," she said. "Wouldn't be the first time."

"Are you in town for the Evans game?"

"I'm here looking for someone." Stepping up a little closer, she added, "Looking for you, Mister Adams."

Clint leaned against the bar. "Well now, it seems my day's looking up."

THREE

The bartender walked over to the table Clint had chosen and set down a pair of mugs filled with beer. When Clint went to his pocket for money, the bartender waved it off. "These two are on the house," he said. "Seeing as how you kept a fight from happening in my place. Those wind up being pretty expensive for the man that's got to replace all them broken chairs and such."

"Thanks," Clint said. He then picked up his mug and held it up to Abigail. She picked hers up and returned Clint's salute before tipping the mug back.

After letting out a grateful sigh, she said, "That's the best thing I've tasted in a while."

"It must have been a long ride getting here," Clint said quietly. "I've seen river water with less silt in it than this beer."

"It's been a long ride through rough country. You're a hard man to find."

"That's funny. I'm not exactly hiding out here."

Abigail set her drink down and took off her hat. She tousled her hair a bit, which set free a pair of braids that had previously been tucked under her collar. The braids were slightly cleaner than the hair that had been outside of the hat, but there was more than enough dust in there to create a gritty cloud around her head as she continued to muss her hair. "You don't have to hide," she said. "There's just plenty of men who are willing to drop your name for any number of reasons."

"Nothing bad, I hope," Clint said as he furrowed his brow.

"Not as such. Most of it's just a bunch of bragging drunks that nobody believes anyway. Still, a few more drunks spread the word and someone a few towns over thinks the Gunsmith is nearby. I got to the genuine article quickly enough."

"I hope you're not disappointed."

"Not yet," Abigail replied with a wry grin.

Clint chuckled and forced down another sip of beer. "So what puts someone like you on my trail?"

"I've got a message from Colonel Farelli. You know of him?"

"Yeah," Clint said with a slow nod. "What's he want?"

"He's been having some Injun troubles and he needed to get word to you as quickly as he could."

"Word about what?"

Abigail shrugged and removed a folded envelope from the pocket of her fringed jacket. "You'll have to read the message for yourself. It's not meant for me."

"You know about the Indian troubles," Clint pointed out.

"Sure, but that's because I had to ride through a range of hills being overrun by Navajo. Some young chief out that way's got his feathers ruffled and he's been sending out raiding parties to attack whatever they can find."

"I've heard about that. Pretty ugly attacks, if I recall."

"You got that right," Abigail said. "Most of the times, the raiders don't even bother stealing anything. They just leave a whole lot of blood so anyone and everyone can see that Tolfox means business."

"Tolfox?"

Nodding once, Abigail said, "Chief Tolfox."

"That's a strange name for a Navajo."

"All their names sound strange to me," she replied with a shrug. "All I know is that riding through that stretch of trail was like running through hell with the devil nipping at my heels. Sitting down to sip from some sandy beer is awfully nice in comparison."

Clint chuckled and took another sip from his own mug. "I know what you mean. After playing cards for days on end without a wink of sleep, I guess I lost some perspective. Are you a friend of Farelli's?"

"No. Why do you ask?"

"Just wondering why he'd send anyone on their own through such dangerous country."

"You mean why he'd send a woman?"

Clint shrugged, but kept his eyes on her. "No offense meant, but it sounds like it would be a tough ride for anyone on their own. I would think an Army man would have plenty of scouts or messengers he could send."

"He sent me because I'm the best for the job," Abigail snapped. "And you don't have to like it."

"Like I said," Clint stated, "there was no offense meant."

Slowly, Abigail nodded and then got back to her beer. She'd set the envelope on the table and now acted as if she could no longer even see it. When Clint reached for the rumpled paper, she recoiled as if she'd been expecting a punch. As soon as she saw what he was doing, she let out a breath and allowed her features to soften. "You were just making conversation," she said. "I shouldn't have bitten yer head off."

"Don't worry about it." When he saw her down the rest of her beer and then push her chair away from the table, Clint added, "You can stay. I could use a bite to eat and you're welcome to join me."

"That's a kind offer, but I think I'll get a room for myself. I saw another saloon down the street had rooms to rent. It'd be the first night I haven't slept on the ground for over a week, so I don't want to risk missing out."

"Maybe later, then," Clint offered.

Abigail smiled and nodded. "Sure. I'd like that."

"What about a late supper?"

"You are a bold one, ain't you?"

"You don't strike me as the sort of woman who'll stay in one place for very long," Clint told her. "And this just happens to be one of the few instances when I can afford to take some time away from the card table."

Having started to walk away from the table, Abigail stopped and turned around so she could look at Clint and say, "Tell you what. If you can track me down later, I wouldn't mind having some supper. I may not have much of an appetite, though."

"I'm a gambling man. I'll take my chances."

FOUR

Clint had heard about the Evans game while spending a night in Tombstone. Like most big poker games, it had taken on a certain mythic quality as word was passed along by the winners and damnations were made by the losers. Also, like most big poker games, it wasn't much more than a collection of gamblers who'd taken to cycling in and out of one continuous event instead of starting a bunch of smaller games. In short, it was just a game that was started up by a man named Evans.

That was it.

The stakes rose and fell, but all the big talk had come about simply because there wasn't much else to talk about of late. Nothing, that is, except for the Indian raids.

Clint had heard about those as well. Coincidentally enough, he took in those stories the same way he'd taken in the ones about the Evans game—with more than a few grains of salt. The reports he'd heard sounded like a string of robberies that may not have even been committed by Indians. Some robbers and a few cowardly souls liked to blame their own deeds on Indians, simply because Indians made for good targets. Other times, there truly were Indians to blame. After all, Indians had their criminals and killers like any other group of people.

For the most part, however, Clint hadn't thought about the attacks one way or the other. He knew he could pick a different route if he needed to ride through that area for a bit and that was all. He was reminded of the incidents as soon as he opened the letter that Abigail had brought to him.

The letter read:

Clint Adams, hopefully this letter finds you in good health and in a short amount of time. Since you must have already heard about the Navajo attacks being launched by Chief Tolfox, I won't go into the bloody details regarding them. Just know that your assistance is needed at a meeting between myself and the chief at the end of this month. It would be greatly appreciated if you could attend this meeting to ensure the safety of my men, since too much of a military display may fan these flames rather than snuff them out. I fear we won't get a second chance at peace talks if this chance goes by. The Navajo are getting bolder and the Army is growing impatient. I hope to settle this matter, but cannot risk losing my men simply because Chief Tolfox insists on keeping the numbers of my negotiators to a minimum. Therefore, I need to ensure the few men I do bring are of the highest quality. Your name came to mind first in this regard and I do hope our past encounters do not prevent you from lending aid in this time of need. At the very least, come to Fort Winstead and hear the rest of my offer. Your service would be greatly appreciated and you will be more than compensated for your time.

Sincerely,
Col. N. Farelli

After reading through the letter, Clint set it down and watched it as if he expected it to pull some sort of trick.

When it did nothing but lay on the table, Clint picked it up and walked over to the bar. The game was still going on at the back of the Jackrabbit Saloon, but was losing steam by the hour. Even so, there were a few men lined up to fill the next chairs that were vacated. As Clint looked toward that end of the saloon, he felt the impulse to go back and reclaim his spot. The letter in his hand kept him from doing so.

"What's the matter, Clint?" the bartender asked as he stepped up to meet him. "This is the longest you've been away from that table for three days. Bad turn of luck?"

"Maybe it just feels good to stretch my legs." When he saw the skeptical glint in the bartender's eye, Clint added, "Okay, so maybe my last few hands weren't the best."

"A bit of rest wouldn't hurt. I've got some nice rooms for rent, you know."

"What do you know about Fort Winstead?"

The bartender winced as if a fly had just buzzed into his ear. "Fort Winstead? Ain't that a long way to go for a night's sleep?"

"I'm not just talking about renting a room, Eddie. I'm talking about anything you might know. I've never even heard of the place."

Throughout most of the Evans game, Eddie had been tending bar. Although Eddie was staying more for the generous gratuities being tossed around by the gamblers, he had the same dark circles under his eyes and the rough edge in his voice as all the others who'd been playing for so long. In that way, it sort of made Eddie a comrade in arms. He blinked a few times and rubbed his face. "Sorry, Clint. I didn't follow you there."

"I guess I could've warned you before I switched tracks like that. You heard of Fort Winstead?"

"Yeah. It's a few days' ride west of here. There were a whole bunch of men driving supplies and wood through here to build the place about a year ago. Big bunch of Army men strutting around and expecting free whiskey because of their uniforms. I'm a patriot and all that, but I still got a business to run."

"Of course."

"Anyway, I've heard it's less of a fort and more of a trading post." Leaning over the bar, Eddie whispered, "Seems that the Federals ran out of money before they were done building the place. I even heard tell that the place was built as a clerical mistake or some sort of swindle."

"A swindle?" Clint chuckled. "What's that supposed to mean?"

Eddie wiped off the top of the bar and shook his head. "I hear a lot of things when I'm serving drinks and that's just one of 'em. There was an Army sharpshooter that passed through not too long ago who had a bit too much beer and started saying all kinds of things. One of them things was that Fort Winstead wasn't even supposed to be built and the Army was too embarrassed to tear it down once they found out where all the supplies had gone. He said all the supplies were supposed to be sold off and nothin' was even built until an officer found out what was going on. Fort Winstead was slapped together with some spit and polish to cover some cheatin' general's ass."

"Or maybe a cheating colonel," Clint grumbled.

"What was that?"

"Nothing. Just putting a few things together. Is there another saloon down the street with rooms for rent?"

When he heard that, Eddie straightened up and glared at Clint as if the honor of his mother and sister were just questioned. "What's wrong with my rooms?"

"Nothing," Clint replied earnestly. "I'd rent one for myself, but not everyone is as anxious to stay so close to all these gamblers."

"Ah! You mean that pretty little gal with the dirt in her hair?"

"The one that nearly cut George off at the knees," Clint added.

"That's the one. She turned right when she stepped out the door, so she's probably headed for Janeway's down the street. That's the only saloon in that direction that rents rooms. Leastways, it's the only one with any rooms left. If that little lady's out to rent a bed that ain't here, she's probably gonna end up there."

"Thanks, Eddie."

"Of course . . . I know my loyal customers wouldn't stab me in the back by—"

"I'll rent one of your rooms for myself," Clint said before Eddie could get around to the same spot.

"And I'll just put it on your account. It's the Presidential Suite at the top of the stairs."

"You had a president stay here?"

"Nope, but it's the fanciest room I got. Worth every penny, too."

"It better be."

FIVE

Judging by the glee on the face of the bartender at Janeway's, that saloon hadn't had many customers walk through their doors for a while. The skinny old man practically jumped from a stool behind the bar and ran toward Clint.

"Welcome to Janeway's," the old man said in a distinct Irish accent. "What can I do for ya?"

"I'm just here to see one of your guests. Has a woman in buckskins just rented one of your rooms?"

The disappointment on the old man's face looked painful. In fact, he practically drooped all the way down to the floor when he swung a tired arm toward a narrow set of stairs. "The rooms are up there," he said. "Are you Clint Adams?"

"Yes, sir."

"Then she's expecting you. Last door on the left."

As he started walking toward the stairs, Clint looked around the saloon to find less than half a dozen people scattered among the tables. "Quiet night, huh?"

"Every night's been quiet since Willie Evans decided to start up his damned game. And don't look at me with no sympathy. I know yer just another one of them gamblers."

Clint looked over the empty tables in the saloon one

more time. Since a good number of those tables were set up for poker and faro, it seemed the old man wasn't entirely opposed to games of chance. "Yeah, well, maybe you should start up your own game. There's no law against that."

Although the old man started to grumble some more sour words, he stopped and furrowed his brow. "You're right. I just might do that."

"Have at it," Clint said as he hurried toward the stairs and climbed them two at a time.

The second floor of Janeway's wasn't much better than the first. It was as empty as it was dusty, although there was a more inviting smell drifting through the air. The closer Clint got to the door the old man had told him about, the stronger that smell became. Finally, he knocked while pulling in a deep lungful of the inviting scent.

"It's Clint Adams," he announced to the door when he didn't get a response. Before he could knock again, the door was pulled open and Clint found himself looking at a vaguely familiar face. "Do I know you?" he asked.

Abigail smiled up at him. Her hat was gone and her hair was mostly loose. Her buckskins were gone as well, leaving only a large towel wrapped around her body to cover her up. Although her skin was still a bit dusty, the warm air that flowed out from the room took away every last trace of the long trail she'd ridden.

"I was about to take a bath," she said. "You got here a lot quicker than I thought you would."

"I could always come back later."

She shrugged and turned around to walk back into the room. Just then, it became obvious that the towel wasn't wrapped around her, but was being held up to cover the front of her body. As soon as she turned her back to Clint, Abigail showed off the finely etched lines of her naked body. Her spine curved along the muscles of her back and led straight down to a firm pair of buttocks that swayed hypnotically as she moved. Abigail's legs were muscled as well, but carried her across the room with a distinctly feminine grace.

Abigail's hair was no longer braided, but hung down past her shoulders in two rows as if it were unaccustomed to being so free. The strands were crooked and a bit knotted, but still soft against the bare skin of her shoulders. After taking a few more steps, Abigail bent down to dip her hand into a bathtub that was filled with steaming hot water.

The towel fell away from her a little more, exposing the finely honed muscle in her hips and thigh. Abigail's naked backside hitched to one side as she bent down further to swirl her hand within the water. As she moved her hand, she slowly moved her hips until the towel was only covering the spot where her other hand was pressing it against her chest.

Standing up to look over her shoulder, Abigail let the towel drop to show Clint the side of one pert breast capped by a pink nipple that was slightly smaller than a penny.

"Then again," Clint said as he stepped inside and pulled the door shut behind him, "I could always stay here to keep you company."

SIX

Clint stepped up behind Abigail as she remained with both hands upon the edge of the tub. Steam rose from the dented metal tub, making it look like a giant stewpot. Despite the poor condition of the tub, which had several slow leaks that contributed to one hell of a puddle on the floor, the scent of that steam was more than enough to make up for it. Soap mixed with a bit of lilac-scented salts to make the entire room smell like a freshly made bed.

But Clint didn't even spare a glance toward the bed. He was doing just fine where he was and he wasn't about to take his eyes off of Abigail's smooth, naked body. He let his hands wander along the slope of her lower back and then down the curve of her hips. From there, he tightened his grip on her and pulled her close against him.

"Oh," she said as she felt the bulge between Clint's legs pressing against her backside. "Seems like someone's getting some mighty big ideas."

"Am I the only one with the ideas?" Clint asked. He reached around to run his hand along her belly and then down between her legs. "Let's just see about that."

Clint's fingers slipped through the downy hair of her pussy and then slid along her moist lips. After a few gentle rubs, her subtle dampness grew wetter and wetter. "Seems like you've got a few notions of your own," he whispered.

"That's just from the bathwater," Abigail replied as she gripped on to the edge of the tub with renewed strength.

"Really?" His fingers slid up and down over her pussy and then settled over her clitoris before making a few quick circles. Clint reached down a bit farther until the palm of his hand was rubbing against her inner thigh. He bent his knees to feel his way down her leg before straightening up and placing his hands back where they'd started. By the time his fingers slid into her, he felt Abigail pressing against him to rub her backside on his erection.

"Maybe I do have an idea or two," she said.

Clint kept one hand between her legs and used the other to unbuckle his belt and ease his jeans down. "Let me guess," he said as he used that hand to guide his cock into her from behind. "Is it anything like this?"

"Oh, yes," Abigail moaned as she leaned forward to accept every inch of him inside her. "That was it, exactly."

Clint took hold of her hips in both hands as he pumped slowly in and out of her. Whenever he buried himself all the way inside, Abigail let out a moan and grabbed on to the tub hard enough to shake the water inside. Soon she held on and tossed her head back to savor every thrust. The moment Clint stopped to catch his breath, she backed against him to pick up where he left off.

While he pulled off his shirt, all Clint had to do was stand still and enjoy the way Abigail rocked back and forth in front of him. She even threw in a few twitches of her hips for good measure. When Clint took a step back, he immediately heard her groan with disappointment.

"Don't worry," he said. "I just need to get my boots off."

Abigail spun around and locked eyes with him. "Be quick about it," she growled as she sat with her backside against the edge of the tub. "You can't keep me waiting after starting like that."

The look on Abigail's face was almost savage. She bared her teeth and spread her legs for him the moment Clint took half a step forward. When she reached out to pull him closer, Clint thought she might just sink a set of claws into him. Abigail pulled Clint by the arm and wrapped her leg around him. She was smiling now and let out a long, relieved sigh when he finally drove his cock into her. She leaned back to brace her hands against the other edge of the tub so her back was suspended above the oval opening.

"You're going to fall in." Clint chuckled.

She shook her head, smiled weakly, and replied, "Don't worry about that. And don't stop. Don't you stop."

Cupping her firm little backside in his hands, Clint held on to Abigail rather than have her perched in such a precarious spot. It also gave him a better angle to drive into her harder and harder as she begged for more. Before long, Clint was holding her completely over the tub as she held on to the edge with both hands behind her back. When he stopped again, Abigail's eyes snapped open.

"What's wrong?" she asked breathlessly.

Looking down at the tub, Clint replied, "I think we moved that thing halfway across the room."

He might have stretched the truth a little, but the tub obviously wasn't in the spot where it had started. Reluctantly, Abigail set her feet down and tried to lean forward. She had barely sat upright before Clint lifted her up and carried her to the bed. Abigail's eyes were as wide as her smile by the time she was set down again.

"Sweeping a lady off her feet?" she mused.

Clint stood in front of the bed as she opened her legs and scooted even closer to the edge of the mattress. "I aim to please," he said.

"Then get back over here and please me."

Abigail wrapped her legs around Clint's waist and locked her ankles behind him. She barely gave him enough time to guide himself into her before pulling him in closer and driving him deeper inside. She leaned back on the bed and stretched out her arms to grab hold of the blankets as Clint picked up his rhythm. The faster he pumped between her thighs, the louder she moaned.

As he thrust in and out of her, Clint reached down to rub a hand along the taut muscles of her thigh. Clint admired the way each inhale brought out the layers of muscle in her trim body and how every exhale set that body to quivering.

Soon Abigail clenched her eyes shut and ground her hips against him. Her climax was powerful enough for Clint to feel as it rippled through her body. While she was still riding that sensation, she looked at him and thrust her hips with a rhythm of her own as if she were the one riding him.

Needless to say, it was one hell of a ride.

SEVEN

Abigail lay in the bathtub with her arms draped along the sides and her head resting on the dented metal edge. Even though she was basically simmering in a giant stewpot, she couldn't stop smiling. "This," she sighed, "is the life."

Having pulled on his jeans, Clint sat on the edge of the bed. Just watching her, he couldn't help smiling either. "It sure is. Now I don't have to look at your dirty face anymore."

Snapping her head around to glare at him, Abigail swatted her hand against the water to send a generous splash his way. "You could always leave, smartass!"

"Not now. After what we just did, you got me all dirty, too."

"Funny, you didn't seem to mind when it was happening."

Walking over to the tub, Clint sat on the edge and looked down at her naked body in the water. "I sure didn't and I don't mind right now. I was just thinking our ride would be a lot easier if we were both clean."

"Our ride?" Abigail asked. "You mean the both of us?"

"Sure. That is, unless you had better plans."

She squinted and grabbed the soap that lay beside the tub. "I thought you were all wrapped up in your card game."

Clint shrugged. "I'm ahead a bit, but a few heavy hitters came into town and are starting to clean up."

"You sure they ain't just cheating?"

"They could be," Clint replied. "Whatever they're doing, they're costing a lot of people a lot of money. I'm not overly fond of Colonel Farelli, but it sounds like he may have a genuine problem."

"What do you have against the colonel?"

"I was doing a favor for a supply sergeant a few years ago. Everything from guns and ammunition to boots and coats were disappearing from a couple different Army posts and I was asked to track down the robbers. Let's just say the robber I found wasn't exactly what the supply sergeant was expecting."

"Farelli?" Abigail asked.

"You got it."

She chuckled and scrubbed at a stubborn spot on one of her forearms. "I bet his hide was tanned something awful."

"Farelli wasn't working alone and one of his partners was ranked high enough to get the matter handled pretty quietly. By the time I left, it looked like the robbers' pay was going to be docked and their records would get a smudge, but that was about it."

"Knowin' them Army fellows, they probably swept it all under the rug because they were embarrassed."

"Probably," Clint said. "Either way, I know Farelli wasn't too happy with me when we parted ways. Come to think of it, he's not exactly my favorite person, either."

"So why would he want to hire you for a job?"

"Because when I caught him red-handed stealing those supplies, he drew a gun on me," Clint explained. "I drew mine faster. A lot faster."

"Did you shoot him?"

After a pause, Clint shook his head. "No, but I could have. He knows it, too. Seeing as how he just got a stiff fine and a blemish on his service record while still making it to colonel, I'd think he came out of it a lot better than if I'd have shot him."

"So maybe the colonel's trying to make up for what happened?"

"I doubt that," Clint said. "This sounds like a dangerous job that could get someone hurt or worse. I'd bet on Farelli wanting to ask me to do it rather than risk his own men. If I come through, he looks like a good leader. If I get hurt . . . well . . . I doubt he'll be heartbroken."

Abigail let out a snorting laugh and said, "I don't see why you'd want any part of a job like this."

"I've heard about these Indian attacks," Clint replied. "Soldiers and innocent folks are getting hurt. I know this is a real thing and Farelli and I both know I could do something to help. If I have to put up with a weasel like Farelli to save some lives down the stretch, I'm willing to grit my teeth and put up with him. If he's trying to pull something else, I'll deal with that, too. I sniffed him out once, and I can do it again. It's not like he was a very good liar anyway."

Nodding as she got back to scrubbing, Abigail said, "That's all well and good, but what if he really is holding a grudge? What if he wants to hurt you for what happened the last time you crossed paths?" The more she thought about it, the more she shook her head. "If I were you, I wouldn't trust a man like him."

"I don't trust him, Abigail. I trust my own eyes, though. I know there's blood being spilled, and if he's stationed at a fort anywhere near those attacks, he'd be the one to deal with them. From what I've seen, I know he'd need help with a job like that."

"And if he's after you?" Abigail asked.

Clint was quick with his reply. "If he's after me, he's got a regiment of fighting men and at least a few among them would follow his orders if he backed them up with enough pay. He'd be able to come after me no matter what I decide to do with this letter."

Although Abigail nodded, she seemed more uncomfortable than agreeable. "Seems like you're not too bothered by someone out to shoot ya."

"Have you ever heard of me before we met?" Clint asked.

"I heard a few stories."

"There you go. I've had men a lot nastier than Farelli coming after me."

"Why do you want me to come along with you?"

"Because you're the best one for the job."

"How do you know that?" she asked suspiciously.

Clint blinked and replied, "Simple. You told me so."

She shook her head and laughed under her breath. "I guess I did."

"The fact of the matter is I've never been to Fort Winstead. All I'd need is a guide there. It would make things a lot easier."

"Fine," Abigail said with a smirk. "I was headed back that way anyhow. I just hope you can keep up with me."

EIGHT

Clint spent the rest of that day wrapping up his business in town. Of course, since he was mainly in town for the game, that business included sitting in on a few more hands to add to his winnings. As it turned out, he lost more than he won. As the sun set and more new faces drifted into the Jackrabbit, the Evans game was taken to new heights. The few locals who still had money left were sitting at the same table with known professional gamblers. Later that night, more tables were added to the mix and the gamblers truly rolled up their sleeves.

The games that followed quickly turned into the poker equivalent of a bloodbath.

Eddie the barkeep shook his head and chuckled as Clint walked up to the bar and supported himself with both hands against the chipped wooden surface. "Not your night?"

Clint looked up and replied, "Let's just say I'm happy to be leaving tomorrow."

That washed away the bartender's smirk real quick. "Tomorrow? What for?"

"Just moving on. By the looks of it, you won't miss having me around."

"It ain't so much the business, but it's dangerous out there. I heard there was another Injun attack."

"What do you know about those?" Clint asked. "How bad was this one?"

"Pretty damn bad. Left four men dead and a few women."

"Jesus."

Eddie nodded solemnly. "A couple wagons headed north got set upon by them damn Navajo."

"Hasn't the Army done anything about it?"

"It won't be long, I'm sure," Eddie replied. "And whenever word gets out about them Injuns being shot down like mangy dogs, it won't be soon enough. Anyways, you weren't headed that way, were you?"

"I was thinking about it," Clint replied. "Now I know for sure."

"Just don't be stupid and you'll be fine. It'd be a shame for the Gunsmith to end his days before he could let everyone know where he played some of the best poker in his life."

Clint rolled his eyes but knew better than to get too bent out of joint by Eddie's request. After all, saloons didn't become famous and poker games didn't become events by printed advertisements. "I'll see what I can do, but there's really not much. You might not like the kind of men that would come running if they knew I might be in a particular saloon."

"I'd be willing to take my chances!"

Rather than continue the debate, Clint paid off what he owed and waved good-bye. Eddie wasn't the first to try and get Clint to draw people to one business or another. There was a fellow who owned a billiard hall in Albuquerque who offered to pay Clint a thousand dollars to talk the place up when he visited California. Then again, that man promptly went broke a few months later. Clint would never stop being surprised at the boneheaded ways some men would try to get rich without breaking a sweat.

After leaving the Jackrabbit, Clint walked over to the livery down the street. He walked straight back to the last stall on the right and found Eclipse, his black Darley Arabian stallion, waiting there patiently as if he'd been expecting the company. "You ready for a run, boy?" Clint asked as he patted the horse's nose.

"He'd better be ready," came a familiar voice from the stall behind him.

Clint jumped and reflexively reached for his gun as he turned around. His hand was still on the grip of the Colt when he said, "That's a good way to get yourself hurt!"

Abigail held her hands up and kicked open the gate to the stall. "If you've got reflexes like that, I feel a lot better about taking this ride with you."

"What in the hell were you doing in there?"

Looking over her shoulder as if she didn't know what Clint could be referring to, she replied, "Checking my horse. I could'a asked who you were talking to, but I didn't."

Clint took a few more steps toward Abigail's stall so he could get a better look inside. The horse in that stall was a white mustang with a few large brown spots on its flank. There was also a saddle buckled in place on its back. "Leaving so soon?" Clint asked.

Once more, Abigail looked around. This time, she didn't pretend to wonder what Clint was talking about. "I just thought I could scout ahead tonight to see if there were any Injun camps nearby. I got a nose for sniffing them out and it'd help us get a good start tomorrow."

"You don't have to guide me. Simple directions to Fort Winstead would suffice. I could even get those from someone else."

"I wasn't gonna leave. I swear!"

Clint nodded and turned to walk away. "Come or go as you please. If you're here in the morning, we can ride together. If not, have a safe trip."

As he walked away, Clint heard an aggravated sigh. He left the livery and walked to the hotel where he'd walked in on Abigail's bath. Even before he approached the front desk, he was being greeted by a prim old lady with a high-collared dress who was now working there.

"Hello, there," she said. Suddenly, her face soured as she glared at Clint through thick spectacles. "Oh. It's you again."

"Have we met?" Clint asked in a friendly tone.

"I meant to bring some more bath salts to the woman upstairs after you went up. I knocked, but you seemed to be . . . busy in there."

Clint shrugged, but he wasn't about to blush. "Oh, well, did that woman check out already?"

"I had her removed," the old lady snapped. "I will not tolerate such lewd behavior in my hotel. And if you see that . . . woman, tell her she still owes me for the water damage done to my throw rug."

While Clint might not be the sort to blush, he did give a little wince when he realized the woman was deadly serious about some rugs getting wet due to some creatively splashed water. Removing some money from his pocket, he slapped it on the desk and asked, "Will that cover the damages?"

Obviously flustered, the old woman said, "Yes, I suppose, but—"

"That's settled, then," Clint interrupted. "You have a good evening, ma'am."

The old woman sputtered a few words and then tried to toss out a few halfhearted thank-yous, but Clint didn't bother looking back as he headed for the door. In fact, after he heard the disgust in the old woman's tone when she'd referred to Abigail, Clint wished a bit more damage had been done to the coot's precious room.

When he got back to the livery, Clint snuck in and found Abigail in the stall with her horse, situating a bedroll in a pile of hay in one corner. "Come on," he said while she was still trying to cover up her blanket. "You're coming with me."

"Where to?" she asked.

"To the most expensive hotel I can find."

NINE

Clint and Abigail woke up fairly early, wrapped in silk sheets. The hotel was actually one town over, but it had been a short ride and was worth every step. They had some sort of fancy omelets for breakfast and washed it down with some ridiculously expensive coffee. Even after taking their time in getting ready, they were in the saddle ahead of schedule. It helped that both of them already had everything stuffed into saddlebags and ready to go.

"You really shouldn't have done all that," Abigail said later that afternoon.

"You mean the breakfast?"

"The breakfast, the hotel, all of it. I would've been fine where I was."

"Sure," Clint replied, "but it wouldn't have been as fun."

She smirked and said, "No, but still . . ."

"Enough," Clint cut in. "Most of that was winnings from the game. I plan on squeezing more than enough from Colonel Farelli to make up for it anyway."

Abigail held her reins easily and glanced over at Clint as she swayed along with every one of her horse's movements. The way she rode made it seem as if she were more comfortable in the saddle than anywhere else. "I haven't known you for long and I already know that's a load of dung."

"Maybe. Does it matter?"

"After sleeping in them sheets and eating that breakfast, it don't matter one bit."

"That's what I thought."

They shared a couple seconds of laughter before Abigail snapped her head around to look in the opposite direction. She stared into the distance with more than enough conviction to put Clint on his guard.

"What is it?" he asked.

But Abigail swung her hand at him in a motion that quickly shut him up. Soon she eased up a bit and then pointed in the same direction she'd been watching. "Someone's coming from that way," she hissed.

"Are you sure? I didn't—" And then Clint heard it.

The sound was faint and he might have missed it if Abigail hadn't already alerted him, but Clint could most definitely hear hooves pounding against the packed earth from that direction. "Could be anyone," Clint pointed out.

Before Abigail said a word, a gunshot crackled through the air. It wasn't a shot fired at them. The shot wasn't even close enough for Clint to be threatened by it. But since there were several more shots that followed it, someone not too far away was very threatened indeed.

Clint and Abigail looked at each other for a moment before both of them snapped their reins. Abigail's mustang got moving first, but Eclipse was hot on its heels.

They were headed up a gradual rocky slope that rose easily toward a jagged edge. As Clint got closer to the edge, he could tell it dropped off steeply on the other side to look down upon an open stretch of sand-covered ground. Gunshots were still being fired and seconds before Clint was close enough to look all the way down to what was happening below, shouts could also be heard.

Clint pulled back hard on his reins to bring Eclipse to a

skidding halt at the edge of the rocks. Abigail was right beside him and leaned so far forward in her saddle that it seemed as if she might fall out. "Aw hell," she said. "Looks like another Injun attack."

The scene below was a chaotic mess of several horsemen weaving among one another, firing their weapons and shouting. Although it was hard to tell who was fighting who, Clint had no trouble picking out the wagon stuck in the middle of it all. One of the two horses in the wagon's team had been killed and was crumpled awkwardly in its rig, while the second horse struggled to keep its footing with all those shots being fired back and forth.

"I can barely tell what's going on down there," Clint replied. "But it sure doesn't look good."

"There's one way to find out!" With that, Abigail pointed her mustang toward a slope that would take her down to the storm that was raging beneath them.

Clint didn't like the idea of charging into a fight without knowing what it was about, but he also didn't know a way to keep Abigail from doing that very thing. "Damn," he grunted as he pointed Eclipse in the direction Abigail had gone and snapped the reins.

TEN

Eclipse's hooves pounded against a surface that became rockier with every step. Loose gravel covered the path in spots, but Abigail's mustang did a nice job of clearing it away seconds before Clint came along. The path leading down to the wagon was narrow enough to require all of Clint's attention to keep from falling off. Once the path leveled out, Clint steered around toward the wagon to find himself immediately thrown into the fray.

There were at least half a dozen men on horseback circling the wagon while tangling with one another. One of those men caught sight of Clint and Abigail, pointed in their direction, and shouted, "They got reinforcements!"

"Kill 'em with the rest!" another of the horsemen replied.

Gritting his teeth, Clint drew his Colt and tried to think of any possible way to make things better rather than worse. In the space of a few seconds, he soaked up as much of the scene in front of him as he could. As far as he could tell, the two riders who'd shouted to each other were dressed in similar jackets that were dirty enough to conceal their color and design. Clint was just quick enough to spot a saber hanging from the belt of one rider before the man circled around the wagon.

The riders that weren't wearing jackets were Indians. They had fire in their eyes and war paint on their faces, but were making less noise than the men they fought. In fact, those quiet Indians set about their task more methodically than all of the white men combined.

In the second or two Clint had taken to gather this information, Abigail had charged in with her gun blazing. She fired at the closest Indian she could find and sent a round hissing through the air over her target's head. The Indian turned in his saddle and aimed a rifle at her that was decorated with feathers and knotted leather. The rifle barked once and spat a round that clipped off a few of the fringes from Abigail's jacket.

Clint took a big risk by digging his heels into Eclipse's sides and charging in front of Abigail. That put him between her and her intended target before she could fire. He prayed that she was thinking clearly enough to keep from pulling her trigger. Rather than keep a closer eye on her, Clint set his sights on the Indian that had fired at her and then pulled his trigger. The Colt bucked against Clint's palm and delivered a bullet that sparked against the Indian's rifle.

The moment the Indian knew his rifle was damaged, he pulled his reins and steered away from Clint and Abigail. There were at least three more Indians to carry on without him.

"Hold your fire!" Clint shouted to Abigail.

She looked at him as if she was about to fire through him rather than around him. "Why?"

"Just follow my lead!"

She didn't look happy about it, but it seemed Abigail would do what Clint asked.

Without staying still long enough to explain himself, Clint rode toward the wagon and fired another round at two Indians who were riding side by side and coming around to approach the wagon from a better angle. Clint fired two rounds in quick succession that didn't draw any blood, but came close enough to break the Indians apart before they could do much of anything. Clint fired another shot that knocked the hat from one of the other riders' heads before he could put a bullet into a retreating Indian's back.

"Who the hell are you, mister?" the closest rider in the jacket asked. "Can't you see there's a fight goin' on?"

"Behind you!" Clint shouted.

Even though there wasn't any immediate danger behind the rider, Clint's warning got the man to duck as Clint fired a round over him. That bullet whipped through the air and sparked against a rock a few feet away from another one of the Indians. The Indian reacted by steering his horse away from the rock and thundering toward the others that were gathering several yards ahead of the wagon.

The man in the jacket who had been approaching Clint straightened up and took a quick look over his shoulder. "Whoever you are, I appreciate the help."

"What's going on here?" Clint asked.

"Damn Injuns attacked this wagon, just like they've been attacking anything else they can find."

A shotgun blast drew everyone's attention back to the wagon. The man who'd fired it was standing up in the driver's seat and waving frantically. "They're gonna make another run at us!" the shotgunner hollered.

"Let's beat them to the punch!" Abigail suggested. Without waiting for word from any of the men, she snapped her reins and led the charge.

The rider who'd been speaking to Clint looked over to notice one of his men slumped in his saddle and struggling to reload his pistol. That left only one other of his riders to contend with the attackers. Looking to Clint, he cursed under his breath and bolted to catch up with Abigail. His remaining partner quickly fell into step alongside him.

Clint steered Eclipse into the middle of the group that consisted of Abigail and the other two riders. As they raced past the wagon, Clint could see the shotgunner and the driver were both armed and firing at the Indians. Clint couldn't do much about those two, but neither man on the wagon seemed to be hitting much of anything anyway.

The first thing Clint noticed once he, Abigail, and the other two men were riding together was that they were the only ones doing any shooting. Ahead, the Indians seemed to be gathering together and waiting for the other men to make their move. They wouldn't have to wait long, since Abigail and the other riders were stampeding toward the Indians with their guns blazing.

Clint kept pace with the others and picked his next targets. Having reloaded his Colt, Clint took careful aim and sent a trio of shots over the Indians' heads. While he made sure none of them were killing shots, one or two of those bullets may have scraped some skin as they went by. He knew they needed to be close if they were to get those Indians to back down.

Two of the Indians flattened their bodies against their horses in response to Clint's shots. Another veered away from the group, and a fourth was twisted around in his saddle as bullets from the others caught him in the chest and stomach. More blood sprayed into the air as another round burned a tunnel through the lead Indian's shoulder. Even though the wound was big enough for Clint to see, the Indian barely even flinched as he sighted down his rifle barrel and returned fire.

One of the riders next to Clint let out a pained groan and fell from his saddle. Clint looked down to see where the man landed and when he looked up again, he saw the remaining Indians turn away from the wagon and race for the surrounding rocks.

"After them!" the lead rider shouted.

Clint pulled back on his reins and said, "You've got a wounded man! Looks like there's two of them!"

Abigail fired at the Indians, but they were already beyond

the range of her pistol. Once she saw the rider that had dropped to the ground, she noticed Clint was slowing down to tend to him. Abigail followed Clint's lead and pulled back on her reins.

The lead rider glanced at the wounded man as well. When he looked back again, he saw the Indians had already built up a head of steam and were practically flying away. In the space of another couple of seconds, the Indians were long gone. "Dammit," he snarled as he gripped his pistol in a hand that trembled with rage. "Dammit all to hell!"

ELEVEN

Clint and Abigail stuck close together and apart from the other men who were gathered around the wagon. As much as he'd wanted to dismount and see what he could do to help, Clint was only waved back by the lead rider and warned to stay put.

"Think we could just get out of here?" Abigail asked.

Clint nodded slowly and replied, "Perhaps, but then we wouldn't know what this was all about."

"It's all over."

"Oh, I wouldn't be so sure about that." As he spoke, Clint fixed his eyes upon the man who was stomping over to him.

The lead rider had enough fire in his eyes to make it look as if he was ready to pull Clint down from Eclipse's back. "You've got a hell of a lot of explaining to do, mister! I've got one man dead and another wounded."

"And your casualties would have been a whole lot worse if we hadn't come around!" Abigail snapped.

The rider glared at Abigail for a moment before shifting his eyes to Clint.

"She's got a point," Clint said with a shrug.

Letting out a frustrated grunt, the man asked, "Who the hell are you two, anyway?"

"I'm Clint Adams and this is Abigail."

Once the man turned his back to Clint and walked over to the rider who'd been recently wounded, Clint climbed down from his saddle and motioned for Abigail to follow him. The other two riders helped the third from his saddle, which was a job that went a lot quicker once Clint rushed forward to help.

"What brought all of this on?" Clint asked as he helped lower the wounded man to the ground.

The lead rider straightened his back and dusted himself off. It only took a few slaps on his shoulders to reveal the Army insignias stitched into his jacket. Now that he was closer to the men, Clint could see similar emblems embroidered onto all of the other men's jackets. The driver and shotgunner tending to the dead horse hitched to the wagon appeared to be civilians.

"What did it look like?" the lead rider asked. "It was an Indian attack."

"So this is an Army shipment?" Clint asked.

The man looked toward the wagon and took another deep breath. It seemed as if an entire day's worth of fatigue settled onto him at that very instant. "Nothing official, but with all the trouble that's been brewing, we've tried to escort as many such wagons as possible. Your help's appreciated, Mister Adams. Both of you did a fine job."

"Good to know we won't be hauled off to a stockade," Clint said.

Putting on a tired smile, the man extended his hand. "The name's Sergeant Davis. If anyone tries to toss either of you into a stockade, you tell them I'll personally have them drawn and quartered."

Clint shook Davis's hand. "Are you stationed out of Fort Winstead?"

"Sometimes. We're part of a special unit that goes where it's needed."

"Just the three of you?"

"There were twelve of us at the start," Davis replied. "It was down to four after a hell of a dustup in the mountains, and now we're down to three."

Following Davis's line of sight, Clint spotted a horse and rider lying in the dirt several paces from the wagon. Both of them were riddled with enough arrows to attach the man to his horse. "Sorry to hear that, Sergeant," Clint said. "Looks like one of those Indians was killed as well."

Davis looked at another body that was stretched out and facedown on the ground. Long, black hair was slick with blood and several bullet wounds were scattered along the Indian's body. "We got one and wounded another," Davis said. "Still doesn't seem like an even trade."

"What were they after?" Abigail asked. "Something that wagon's carrying?"

"Who the hell knows?" Davis replied. "As soon as we spotted them, they let their arrows fly and killed Aberman on the spot. When they came down to finish us off, we put up more fight than they were probably expecting, and then you two showed up."

"He's hurt bad, sir," the young rider who was attending to the wounded man said. By the looks of him, he must have been in his teens when he'd first put on his uniform. Although this obviously wasn't his first fight, he looked more like a boy than a soldier.

Davis knelt down beside the wounded man and peeled open his jacket. Underneath the standard issue clothing there was a bullet hole through the man's ribs and a whole lot of blood. "You won't be getting a ticket out of this outfit just yet," Davis said. "But we'll need to get you to a doctor. Do you know where we could find a doctor nearby, Adams?"

Before Clint could say a word, Abigail said, "There's one in the town we just came from. I saw the office across the street from that fancy hotel."

Clint nodded. "It's the Turquoise Hotel," he said. "You can't miss it."

"Right across from that hotel. I saw the doctor plain as day," Abigail said. "That's the only one I know but there could be more."

Davis and the younger soldier were already pressing wadded material against the wounded man's side and lifting him up. "That'll do just fine, ma'am. We should be able to find it."

"Do you need any help getting him there?" Clint asked.

"No. You've done more than enough already. We can handle the rest."

Clint stepped forward and spoke to Davis in a quick whisper. "I'm not blind. Your men are hurt and you've got a wagon being pulled by a dead horse. I'm not trying to tell you how to run your unit, but at least take the help we're offering."

It was clear that Davis meant to refuse Clint again outright. But then the sergeant took a moment and nodded. "The driver can get that carcass from the rig and be on his way, but they'll be too busy to watch for any Indians that decide to circle back."

"I can help with the work and Abigail can keep watch," Clint offered.

"If you see anything, fire into the air and we'll come back," Davis insisted.

Clint nodded quickly. "Fine. Great. Now get moving before you lose another man today."

"Are you a military man, Adams?"

"No, sir."

"Well, you could've fooled me." Judging by the look in Davis's eyes and the tone in his voice, he couldn't have paid Clint a bigger compliment. He turned around and helped the wounded man along, leaving Clint with the wagon. "You get rolling as soon as you can, Mackie," he shouted.

The driver was busy trying to pry the dead horse from the rig, so he simply waved and hollered, "Will do."

Abigail looked back and forth between Clint and Davis so many times, it seemed she might have gotten dizzy. "So what do we do now?" she asked.

Clint rolled up his sleeves and walked toward the wagon. "I'm going to try to move that dead horse. You watch for any Indians that try to kill me while I'm at it."

TWELVE

With the wagon driver, shotgunner, and Clint working at it, the dead horse was eventually removed from the rig. The remaining horse seemed so grateful to be able to stand up straight again that it didn't mind pulling the wagon on its own. Fortunately, the wagon was light enough to make its way without the other horse for a while.

Climbing back into his own saddle, Clint asked the driver, "You sure you're going to be all right?"

"Yeah." The driver sighed. "We'll have to go a bit slower than before, but Sergeant Davis won't let us go too long on our own. I think them Injuns were mainly after them Army fellas anyways."

"What makes you say that?"

"We traveled a long way on our own before meeting up with that armed escort. We even passed some Injuns a few times and they didn't do anything but watch us pass. Soon as them Army fellas joined us, the redskins sat up and took notice."

"Is that so?"

The driver wiped some sweat from his brow and cast his eyes along the horizon. "Truth be told, I didn't keep a journal on it, but that's how it seemed to go for me. I'd also rather not stand about and talk it over. We should really be moving."

"Where you headed?" Clint asked.

"We're bound for a trading post a couple days west of here."

"Care for an escort?"

"Seeing as how you're not wearin' uniforms, we should be just fine," the driver replied as he climbed into his seat and gathered up his reins. The shotgunner sat beside him quietly. So far that one hadn't let more than a word or two pass his lips.

Clint settled into his own saddle and motioned toward Abigail, who was keeping watch from higher ground. "You really think those Indians were after the Army men, then?"

"Hell, I don't know. I just know when we got ambushed. For all I know, them redskins could've been waiting for us to get to this spot the whole time or they might've made their move before more soldiers arrived. Could've been some bad firewater in their veins. I'll contemplate it all once I've got my feet up and this wagon is where it needs to be."

"Fair enough," Clint said. "Lead the way."

The driver flicked his reins and let out a few yelps, but it didn't take much to get the horse moving. The horse seemed more than ready to get away from its dead partner, but it took an awful lot of pulling to get the wagon moving. Once the wheels were rolling, however, the horse fell into an easy rhythm and got going along the trail.

Clint rode alongside the wagon and was soon joined by Abigail. "So we're keeping watch over this one now?" she asked.

"Just until the sergeant comes back."

"Won't be no need for that." Since those words came from the shotgunner, they caught everyone's notice.

The driver, Clint, and Abigail all looked toward the previously quiet man. The shotgunner nodded toward the south and then shifted his weapon so it was propped against his hip.

Looking in the direction the shotgunner had indicated, Clint saw a row of figures skylined upon a nearby ridge. There were three men sitting tall in their saddles. Although they were a bit far for Clint to make out the riders' faces, he didn't have any trouble spotting the feathers hanging from their head and armbands, as well as the rifles that were on prominent display.

"No sudden movements," Clint said. Although the shotgunner was content to remain in his spot, Clint could feel the anxiousness boiling to his left. "That goes double for you," he said to Abigail, who was practically jumping from her saddle.

"You wanna get into another fight with them Injuns?" she asked.

"No. That's why I don't want anyone to make any sudden moves."

She complied, but obviously wasn't happy about it.

Clint knew she might not sit still for long, so he reached into his saddlebag as best he could without making any moves that might be taken the wrong way from anyone watching him from afar. He found the spyglass with ease and pulled it from the saddlebag. Placing the lens to his eye, Clint got a closer look at the horsemen watching them from the ridge.

"More redskins?" the driver asked.

"The same ones from before," Clint replied. "They're watching us."

"Look like they might take another run at us?"

After studying the Indians for a few more seconds, Clint shook his head. "I don't think so. They've got rifles and they could have fired at us already."

"They're in a perfect spot for it," the shotgunner pointed out.

Focusing on one of the Indians in particular, Clint said,

"You got that right. If they wanted to, they could have started firing and probably hit at least one of us by now."

Abigail was getting anxious again. "So what do we do?"

"Keep moving," Clint replied. "Nice and easy."

The next few seconds went by like a stone sinking into molasses. Clint watched the Indians every step of they way. As he did, it seemed as if the lead Indian watched him just as closely, but without the aid of a spyglass. In fact, Clint felt as though that Indian could look him straight in the eye from several miles away.

After the wagon had cleared the ridge and moved into an open stretch of land, the driver asked, "Are they followin' us?"

"No," Clint replied. "They're gone."

"I appreciate you stayin' close. We should be fine from here on."

"You sure about that?"

"That was a prime spot for an ambush," the shotgunner said. "There ain't another spot like it between here and where we need to go."

Clint would have liked to stay with the wagon for a bit longer, but he could tell by looking in the shotgunner's eyes that he wasn't going to let his guard down anytime soon. "All right, then," Clint said as he tipped his hat. "We'll be moving along. You men take care."

"Right back at ya," the driver replied. "Thanks again."

After Abigail and Clint had put some distance between themselves and the wagon, she leaned over and asked, "You think they'll be okay on their own?"

"They won't be on their own for long. Davis or that other soldier will be along shortly. Besides, I have a feeling we'll be able to do a lot more good if we hurry up and get to Fort Winstead."

THIRTEEN

Clint was glad Abigail was along for the ride. Without her, he might have had a hard time finding Fort Winstead. As far as forts were concerned, Winstead wasn't much. Its walls were higher on one side than the other, and had gaps between the logs that were filled in with everything from sod to rocks. A flagpole stretched above everything else, but wasn't flying any colors. When Clint and Abigail approached the front gate, they might as well have been riding up to a run-down trading post.

"You sure this is the place?" Clint asked.

Abigail nodded. "It ain't much to look at, but this is the place all right. The officers are in that building over there."

Looking at the spot Abigail was pointing at, Clint found a shack with a broken window.

There were plenty of folks milling about within the walls of the fort. About half of them were dressed as soldiers and the other half appeared to be a mix of families and shopkeepers. For a small town, the place wasn't too bad. The shops seemed to be prospering. There was a blacksmith in a well-stocked shop of his own. Two stables were filled with horses and a livery was available to tend to the needs of bigger wagons. In the short ride from the gate to the officer's shack, Clint was able to get a close look at several soldiers. Their uniforms were rumpled and their faces were unshaven. One or two of them may have even been drunk.

"What do you know about the colonel?" Clint asked.

Abigail shrugged. "I barely met the man. I got the job, he handed the letter to me and told me to make sure it got to you."

"What's your impression of him?"

"Honestly?"

Looking over to make sure he had a good view of her eyes, Clint replied, "Honestly."

"Whenever he can't get out of doin' something, he does the least it takes to get it done. If he hadn't paid me so much to get you here, I would've gone a mile out of my way just to make sure I didn't see him." When she saw the expression on Clint's face, she added, "Well, you told me to be honest."

"I sure did. Looks like this is the place," Clint said as he brought Eclipse to a stop in front of the shack. "You want to come in?"

"Hell yes. The colonel still owes me half my payment. I was supposed to get my money from one of his men at another post, but I think I'd rather see him personally."

"That may be a good idea."

Those words had barely come out of Clint's mouth when the shack's door was pulled open. Clint's hand was poised to knock, so he pulled it back and extended it to the man who'd opened the door.

"Hello. My name's Clint Adams. I believe Colonel Farelli is expecting me."

The man at the door was in his twenties and the closest thing to a real soldier Clint had seen since he'd gotten to the fort. His face and uniform were all composed of straight lines and perfect angles. When he looked at Clint, his face might as well have been carved from granite.

"The colonel's inside," the man said without shaking Clint's hand. He then stepped past Clint and tipped his hat curtly to Abigail. "Ma'am."

Abigail let the young man pass and then fell into step behind Clint so she could shut the door after both of them were inside.

Colonel Farelli wasn't hard to find. The shack had one room and most of it was filled by a large desk that had most definitely seen better days. The edges of the desk were chipped and the top was piled high with papers and writing implements. The man behind the desk wore an Army uniform that had just enough ribbons to show Farelli's rank. The boots he'd propped on top of a smaller stack of papers must have been polished within the last hour.

"Colonel Farelli?" Clint asked.

But the colonel had his sights set upon Abigail. "I didn't expect to see your pretty face around here so soon, Abby."

Abigail grinned unconvincingly and shrugged her shoulders. "After I gave Clint your message, he asked me to show him back. I was headed this way and I thought . . ."

"You thought you'd go the extra mile, huh? Very admirable."

"I was hopin' to be movin' along soon," she added. "You think I could get the second half of my payment?"

"Why don't I give you what you want after a nice dinner?" Farelli asked as he got to his feet and circled his desk.

Without batting an eye, Abigail said, "I'd like the money now, thanks."

Farelli nodded slowly and scowled. When he looked at Clint, it was only for a moment before swiftly turning back around and snatching a pencil from his desk. "Take this to the quartermaster," he said while scribbling on a piece of paper. "He hands out the pay as well."

Abigail accepted the paper but was careful to look it over carefully.

"It's all there," Farelli snarled. "Take it and go."

She tucked the paper into a pocket and looked to Clint. "I'll be stocking up on supplies before I head out," Abigail said. "You can find me if you want."

"I'll be sure to do that," Clint replied. "Don't go anywhere until I can buy you a drink."

That seemed to brighten her mood a bit. Abigail's grin only lasted until her eyes swept over the spot where Farelli was leaning against his desk and staring at her. "Colonel," she said quickly.

"Don't be a stranger, Abby," Farelli said, making sure to refer to her in a way that obviously didn't set well with Abigail. Once she was gone, he looked at Clint as if he'd been alone in his shack until that very moment.

FOURTEEN

"Hello, Farelli," Clint said.

Extending his hand, he announced, "It's Colonel Farelli now. Good to see you decided to come."

Clint shook Farelli's hand, noticing the colonel's distinct effort to exert some force in his grip. The handshake was enthusiastic, but not very impressive. "We've met, sir," Clint replied. "I'm sure you recall."

"Oh, I sure do. But that was before . . ." Releasing his grip, Farelli proudly tapped the rank insignia on his shoulder.

"That's right. Congratulations."

Beaming like a kid who'd just won the spelling bee, Farelli marched behind his desk and sat down. He then motioned toward one of the other chairs in the room and said, "Have a seat, Adams. I'll get right down to the heart of the matter, since I'm sure you've already heard about the Indian attacks that have been happening of late."

"Heard about them and seen them for myself."

"Really? Nothing too serious, I hope."

"Actually, it was on the way over here," Clint replied while carefully studying Farelli's reaction. "Abigail and I crossed paths with a wagon being guarded by a Sergeant Davis. Do you know of him?"

Farelli wasn't too hard to read. He was smug when Clint began his story, but his expression turned to one of surprise when he heard Davis's name. "He came through here not too long ago. Did he mention me?"

"No. Should he have mentioned you?"

Pulling himself together with a few breaths, Farelli puffed out his chest and regained his original smugness. "We're both dealing with the same problem. The reason I requested to speak to you was so you could help us with that problem. I've arranged to meet with Chief Tolfox. He runs the tribe that's been responsible for most of the attacks, so I hope to smooth over enough differences to ensure the safety of travelers in this area."

"Are you sure this chief has a problem with the travelers?" Clint asked. "What if he's just attacking the men in uniform?"

"If that's the case, it's the first I've ever heard of it. Besides, I can only know about the attacks that are brought to my attention and those have been the ones involving Army men."

Clint knew it was pointless to pursue that matter any further. If Farelli was hiding something, he wasn't about to give it up. Even if he wasn't hiding anything, what he'd said fell well within the realm of possibility. Clint had to forget about who he was dealing with and focus on the task at hand. "Where do I come into this?" he asked.

"I thought the letter was clear. Since my men have been under fire, I assume this Chief Tolfox is keeping watch for them. At the very least, it's safe to assume he's got men among his warriors who have a knack for hunting down the Army uniform."

"That seems about right."

Settling into a whole other layer of smugness now that he

saw Clint was genuinely paying attention, Farelli leaned back in his chair and said, "Going to these peace talks with a brigade of armed men wouldn't send the proper message and might just spark a fight straightaway. If I don't send enough armed men, I'd be putting my negotiators at risk. That's why I need to send a few extremely capable men to the talks. Since you were in the area and you can handle yourself under such conditions, I thought I'd ask for your help."

"Are you going to the talks?" Clint asked.

That question hit Farelli like a cold slap in the face. "No. My relations are . . . strained with Tolfox. My presence there wouldn't be prudent."

"Of course not. Who will be going?"

"If all goes well, you'll be going along with my second in command as well as a few of my assistants who are qualified to barter a certain amount of our goods if that should be necessary."

Clint chuckled under his breath. "Trying to buy them off?"

Farelli held out both hands and replied, "Whatever works. I'd just like to be done with this whole mess. If you don't want to take part, that's fine. If you do, you'll be paid a fee of five hundred dollars to cover your expenses as well as the services you're providing."

Oddly enough, that moment was the first time when Clint didn't suspect anything from the colonel. He already knew Farelli was a conniving weasel, but he seemed well intentioned enough as far as this job was concerned. After all, the man still was an Army officer, and he had a job to do.

"Can I think about it?" Clint asked.

"Sure. You've got until tomorrow."

"That's not a lot of time."

"You're not the easiest man to track down," Farelli shot back. "Johnson is the man to see at the bunkhouse. He'll set you up with a place to stay, if you like."

Clint started to leave the room, but stopped before opening the door. Turning toward Farelli's desk, he asked, "What's your angle?"

"Pardon me?"

"The last time we met, you were being charged with stealing supplies and pocketing the profits. Now you make me this offer, complete with five hundred dollars and a free room for the night. Surely you might have expected I'd be a little suspicious."

Although Farelli kept his posture straight and his chin high, the expression on his face dropped all the way to his boots. His eyes burned for a moment before sputtering out. "You caught me red-handed, Adams. I was fined and prosecuted. It's over. You can help put a stop to this bloodshed, so you can either do it or not. It's too late for much of anything else that used to be between us."

Clint hadn't seen that coming. Farelli actually seemed honest. "All right. I'll help out." Placing his hands upon the edge of the desk, Clint leaned forward and added, "But if I so much as sniff the first hint of a double-cross, I'll make sure you'll regret ever seeing my face again."

"Fair enough. The bunkhouse is out my door and to your right."

FIFTEEN

Clint walked out of the shack and meant to look around for Abigail before heading to the bunkhouse. As luck would have it, both of his searches were ended with one casual glance. Abigail was leaning against the bunkhouse.

She waited for him to approach before asking, "Was that asshole like that when you got him locked up?"

"Pretty close, yeah."

"Good."

"Did you get your money?" Clint asked.

Patting her jacket pocket, Abigail replied, "Every cent, and I sure as hell ain't spending any of it in this place. If you're headed west, I'd be willing to show you a few more sights."

"I'm staying here for the night. After that, I'm joining Farelli's second in command to meet with the chief of the tribe that's been attacking folks around here."

"You're really working for that colonel?" Abigail asked with shock written across her face. "How can you trust a damn word he says?"

"I don't," Clint replied. Glancing around to notice that a few men in uniform were approaching, he lowered his voice and leaned closer to her. "And I don't have to trust him. If he meant to set me up for a fall, this is the perfect mission for it. From everything I've seen about this Indian situation, things couldn't be much worse.

"For a man like the colonel, the first move he'd make is to send an enemy or expendable annoyance into this fight. He might be stretching the truth to bring me here, but this is something I'd want to do no matter what. There're good men dying and I think I can help fix that. I've had some experience with the Navajo and I may be able to ease things up a bit, or at least find out what's causing all of this so I can get that information to someone who actually does his job properly."

Abigail chuckled humorlessly and asked, "You think the colonel is just stretching the truth?"

"He may be lying about a lot of things, but the fact of the matter is that he may be the one behind this and the best way for me to find out is to spend a few days with his men and see what I can see. I'm not stupid enough to let him or any of the soldiers in his pocket get close to me."

"You're stupid enough to sleep in his bunkhouse," Abigail pointed out. "That snake in the grass might just slit yer throat before you wake up."

Clint shook his head and waited for another couple of Army men to pass by. Even though they didn't seem interested in what he was saying, Clint waited for the soldiers to pass. "We butted heads, but Farelli came out of it smelling like a rose. He's got a promotion and he seems perfectly happy running this place into the ground. He's a pig in slop and the worst he's probably got lined up for me is to throw me to some angry Indians that he doesn't realize are on good terms with me. Whether he knows it or not, I'm suited for this job. If I could've arranged to meet with the Navajo to stop this bloodshed on my own, I would've done it."

"Even if Farelli had to be involved?"

"Even if he was to be involved," Clint assured her. "He

doesn't even want to come along for this meeting, which fits perfectly with what I already know about the man."

"So you just want to try and do this job right whether the colonel wants it that way or not?"

"That's right."

She shook her head, but then started to laugh uncomfortably. "Yer a hell of a brave man or a damn stupid one," she said. "At least yer heart's in the right place."

"I appreciate that . . . I think. Whichever kind of man I am, I don't want you coming along with me for this job."

"I wasn't about to ask," she quickly replied. "If I wanted to lock horns with every tribe this side of the Rockies, not even the great high and mighty Gunsmith could talk me out of it."

Clint reached out to slide his hand around the back of her head so he could pull her close. No matter how much Abigail tried to strut and snarl like a fighter, she melted against him the moment she felt her lips touch his. Her face was dirty as always, but her skin was soft to the touch. After he let her go, Abigail needed a moment to rebuild her hardened exterior.

"Take care of yourself, Abigail. Don't get in over your head."

"The same goes for you, Adams," she said as her hand drifted quickly between his legs. "And next time we cross paths, I'll take care of you."

SIXTEEN

Clint spent the rest of that day waiting for something to happen. He got situated in his bunk and waited for someone to approach him about the next day's events. He ate supper with the rest of the soldiers and had a beer at the small saloon that was set up in what appeared to have been an old blacksmith's tent. He went to sleep expecting to be approached by Farelli or one of his assistants and he woke up wondering if he'd been forgotten somewhere along the line.

Not only was Clint left alone, but he was completely ignored. It seemed the rest of the men had plenty to do between their own duties and the daily affairs that were required to keep the fort running. When something actually did happen, Clint was almost startled enough to jump.

"Mister Adams?" a young man in a private's uniform asked.

Clint was buckling up his saddlebag when the younger man approached his bunk. "That's me."

"You're the one that supposed to ride out with Lieutenant McGurn?"

"Where's the lieutenant heading?"

The young soldier blinked and replied, "To meet with those Indians, sir."

"Then I'm the one you're looking for," Clint replied.

Nodding as if he was on the wrong side of a bad joke, the private said, "I'm to show you to the stable, then. All of us are about to leave."

"What about Colonel Farelli?"

"He won't be coming with us, sir. Actually, I think he's still asleep."

Lowering his voice a bit, Clint asked, "Kind of a late sleeper, huh?"

The private chuckled and nodded. "Nobody's ever seen him any earlier than ten o'clock. Some of us call him Cold Brew on account of he's never in the canteen until the coffee's cooled off." Suddenly, the private's grin faded and he straightened up. "But . . . um . . . it wouldn't be a good idea to . . . I mean . . ."

"Don't worry," Clint assured him. "I won't let Cold Brew know he's called anything but Colonel."

"I appreciate that, sir."

"If you're riding with me today, you might as well call me Clint."

The soldier grinned again, which made him look more like a kid than anyone suited to wear a uniform and carry a rifle. "Clint, it is. Are you really Clint Adams, sir? The Gunsmith?"

"That's what some folks call me."

"We've heard about some of the things you've done. That is, me and some of the others stationed here. Some of the stories are pretty impressive."

"Most stories are. And I don't appreciate people telling stories about me," Clint said sternly. "Especially when they don't even take the time to introduce themselves properly."

At first, the private seemed taken aback by Clint's change of tone. Then he relaxed when he realized what Clint was truly after. "I'm Private Biggs," he said as the spark came back to his eyes. "Emory Biggs."

"Nice to meet you," Clint said amicably. "Feel free to tell all the stories you want."

Biggs turned and headed for the front of the bunkhouse. "Yes, sir. You know where the stable is?"

"Sure do."

"The rest of us will be there and intend on leaving as soon as possible."

"I won't hold you up," Clint said as he hefted his saddlebag onto his shoulder and left his bunk behind. "I'm ready to go."

Biggs was a tall kid who walked as if he didn't truly know how long his legs were. His head naturally bowed to nearly every other soldier he passed, since only a few of the buglers and drummers were below him in the military pecking order. Despite his mannerisms, Biggs never seemed timid. He already spoke to Clint as if they were old friends.

"Some of us didn't think it would really be you that came along for this," Biggs said. "We figured ol' Cold Brew was just trying to get our spirits up by saying he was sending the Gunsmith along with us and then he would throw in some hired gunfighter at the last second."

"Is that something he does a lot?" Clint asked.

Biggs paused for a second and then replied, "No, but it's the sort of thing he'd be likely to do. One time he sent out a patrol and told them they'd meet up with another infantry unit. There wasn't no infantry out there. It was all just smoke to get us to where we needed to be."

"I'll bet you came back pretty quickly after that."

"Hell yes, sir," Biggs said. Seeing that he was getting closer to a bunch of other men, he lowered his voice and said, "We sure did. I suppose that was the point. I've never heard of a commanding officer doing things like that, but I suppose it worked."

"Yeah." Clint sighed. "I suppose it did."

The stable felt crowded, but that was mainly because hardly any of the stalls were filled and most of the other space was filled. Several men and their horses were packed into the aisle between the two rows of stalls, going through the last bits of preparation before saddling up. When Clint and Biggs walked into the stable, every last man stopped what they were doing so they could get a look for themselves.

There was a moment of heavy silence, which was broken by a question asked by a scruffy cowboy toward the back of the aisle. "That really Clint Adams?" he asked.

Of all the men inside the stable, only Biggs and one other were in uniform. The soldier with the larger collection of ribbons on his chest said, "That's him. I've seen him before in Dallas as well as Labyrinth."

Clint squinted into the shadows within the stable and then smiled. "Sid McGurn? I didn't expect to see you again."

McGurn stepped forward and extended his hand. "Probably not, especially since I could barely put two cents together for a slice of bread the last time we met." Turning to the rest of the men, McGurn added, "Don't ever play poker with this one. He'll cheat you blind!"

Clint rolled his eyes and waved off the warning. He was then introduced to the other three men who followed McGurn's lead by slapping Clint on the shoulder or throwing him a few lighthearted threats about cheating at cards. One of the men was a scout. Another was along to translate Indian languages and the third was armed to the teeth. Apparently, Clint wasn't the only one coming along for protection.

"Is this the whole bunch?" Clint asked.

McGurn nodded. "It is, but our scout will only come for a portion of the ride to make sure we're heading in the right direction. After that, we're on our own."

"Suits me," the gunman replied. "I got enough bullets to clean out the whole tribe."

"Let's not make that our first plan," Clint suggested. "Things might go a whole lot smoother that way."

McGurn led his horse from the stable and immediately climbed into the saddle. "Agreed. Our orders are to attend this meeting and work out a truce. Only if that fails do we fire a shot. Understood?"

The men sounded off as they emerged from the stable and mounted up. Clint brought Eclipse out last and noticed that McGurn was watching him intently. "I don't get extra pay for getting myself killed," Clint said. "I'd be happy with just watching you boys talk."

Nodding and pointing his horse's nose toward the fort's front gate, McGurn said, "All right, then. Let's ride."

SEVENTEEN

The men rode with a purpose and McGurn led them as if they were headed into a war. After a few pleasantries were exchanged outside the fort, the group thundered to the north and didn't let up their pace for hours. They didn't push the horses to their limits, but they rode without a few words passing between them.

The scout had bolted ahead of them before the rest of the horses could hit their stride and didn't show his face again until well past noon. When he caught sight of the scout, McGurn motioned for the rest of the men and then pulled back on his reins. The group slowed as one, allowing the scout to catch up and fall into step alongside McGurn.

"They're waiting for us about two miles ahead," the scout said. He was breathing heavily enough to make it seem as if he'd done most of the running instead of his horse. "About a dozen of them."

McGurn nodded once and asked, "Are they setting up an ambush?"

"I don't think so. From what I could see, it looks like they're just waiting. There's a tent set up and everything."

Setting his jaw into a firm line, McGurn let out a breath and slowly looked along the horizon in front of him. "Biggs and I will ride ahead. I want the rest of you to spread out and follow us in. We're supposed to be going in under the banner of peace, so I don't want any guns drawn. Keep your hands in the open, but be ready to draw. Understand?"

"Yes, sir!" Biggs replied.

The rest of the men simply nodded or grunted a few words. Clint belonged to the first group.

The scout, on the other hand, fidgeted uncomfortably in his saddle. "I won't be going any further," he said. "I was supposed to make sure nobody snuck up on you men along the way and that's what I did. Colonel Farelli said I could—"

"I know what he told you," McGurn interrupted. "If you intend on leaving, then just go."

Glancing around at the men, the scout turned his horse toward the west and snapped his reins. Judging by the way he spurred his horse, he wasn't about to stay in the area for one second longer than he'd been paid to.

McGurn made a quick waving motion, which was enough to set the rest of the men into motion. He snapped his reins and held his spot at the front of the group.

Breaking the command he'd just been given, Clint rode up to a spot on McGurn's left. Private Biggs nearly jumped across the lieutenant to try and shove Clint back.

"It's all right, Biggs," McGurn said. Turning to Clint, he asked, "Something on your mind, Adams?"

"Were you planning on going ahead with just Biggs to guard you?" Clint asked.

"Nolan knows his orders. He'll be enough to get us out if things go bad."

Nodding toward the man who wore a double-rig holster along with a Winchester strapped across his back, Clint asked, "Is that Nolan?"

"It sure is," McGurn replied.

"With all due respect, I think I'd like to be the one to go along with you."

For the first time since the ride had begun, McGurn

broke out of his official demeanor and became more of the man that Clint had beaten at poker. "Why do you say that?"

"It's why I came along. I don't think Farelli went through all that trouble to find me just so I could hang back and watch for things to go badly. I can do a lot more good if I'm in the middle of things."

"I respect you, Clint, but I don't know why Farelli would go through so much trouble to hire you. Some of us thought you'd be replacing Nolan altogether, but that's not how it turned out."

"Why would Nolan be replaced?"

"You ask a lot of questions, Clint."

"It's a quick way to find out things," Clint replied.

"What sort of things?"

"That you don't hold the colonel in very high regard, for one."

McGurn snapped his head around to shoot a quick look at Private Biggs. Reflexively, Biggs looked away and steered his horse to one side to give the lieutenant some room.

"Where'd you come up with that?" McGurn asked in a low voice that could barely be heard over the sound of hooves against the earth.

"You twitch when you call him by his rank and have already started calling him by his common name. And even when you do that . . . you still twitch," Clint explained.

"Still got an eye for twitches, huh?"

"That's how I've won so many hands of poker," Clint said. "Also, you conduct yourself like a proper soldier. Any man who acts befitting his rank would have a problem with someone like Farelli. How the hell did he get to be an officer anyway?"

"Lord only knows, but he is the one issuing the commands," McGurn said. "Since he's actually doing something to try and stop these attacks before they get any worse, I'm inclined to follow his lead."

Already seeing the smoke from the fires of a nearby

camp, Clint spoke quicker before they got any closer to the awaiting Indians. "Doesn't the Army have someone better than him to handle this?"

"Farelli handled a group of unruly redskins when he was awaiting a formal court-martial. I believe you know something about that."

"You're damn right, I do."

"Farelli came up with a plan to deal with the Indians and they would only talk to him. Blood was being spilled and he was about to go on the block anyway, so he was allowed to try his own plan. It worked and he slipped away from his court-martial with a slap on the wrist. He even got promoted," McGurn added with a shake of his head.

"Sounds like you know a lot about the subject."

"I looked into it after I was stationed here. I had to know how a man like that could be in command."

"And you still take his orders on this?" Clint asked.

McGurn nodded solemnly. "This is a job that needs doing, no matter who gives the order to start the work. I assume that's the same reason you're along for this ride."

"Pretty much," Clint said. "Should I fall back?"

After deliberating for all of two seconds, McGurn barked, "Nolan, you stay back and watch to make certain we don't get flanked while we're in the meeting."

"But you can't just go in there with the kid!" Nolan protested.

"I won't be. Adams is coming with me and Biggs."

"But—"

McGurn snapped his head around quickly enough to rattle almost every decoration on his hat and jacket. "You have a problem with that, mister?"

Even though Nolan was carrying enough guns to supply the entire group, he reflexively backed off when he saw the fire in McGurn's eyes. "I guess not. You're the officer, but Farelli will hear about this."

"Then he'll hear it from both of us, because everything will wind up in my report." With that, McGurn set his sights upon the group of Indians watching him from a small camp less than a hundred yards away. "All right, men. We know what to do. Let's do it and get home in time for supper."

•

EIGHTEEN

Since Clint had succeeded in changing McGurn's arrangement, the group of soldiers filed into the Indian camp in a different order than planned. To an outside observer, however, there was no hitch in the Army men's operation. On the outskirts of the camp, Nolan reined his horse in and stopped to watch the rest of the men proceed. Private Biggs stopped short of the main tepee in the middle of the camp while McGurn was escorted the rest of the way by Clint and the translator.

Clint hoped to spot anything out of the ordinary that might help give him an edge in whatever was coming, but there simply wasn't much to see. There were plenty of Indians—Navajo, by the looks of them—and they watched the Army men with as much suspicion as anyone might expect. There were plenty of rifles, spears, and bows on display, but none of them were aimed directly at the camp's visitors. Just as McGurn drew to a stop, a trio of men stepped from the tepee.

Two of the men were obviously warriors. They carried their weapons as if they were part of their bodies and didn't need to wave them in any threatening manner. They were also built like brick walls, with enough muscle to make it seem like they could punch out a horse. The third man wore the robe and headdress of a chief. He appeared to be somewhere in his forties, but had a youthfulness that made his age difficult to judge. There was also something that set him apart from the rest of the Indians at that camp. For the moment, Clint couldn't quite put his finger on what that was.

"We're here to speak to Chief Tolfox," McGurn announced.

The man between the two braves looked at the lieutenant with crystal-clear eyes and nodded once. He then turned and stepped back into the tepee.

"Come inside," one of the braves said. "Leave your weapons."

Although McGurn and the translator reached for their gun belts, Clint stood his ground. "Will you be leaving your weapons outside?" he asked.

The brave squinted as if he was considering crushing Clint under his foot.

"If these are supposed to be peace talks, we should all talk peacefully," Clint explained. "Otherwise, any man would be foolish to let himself be surrounded and weaponless."

"The white man's Army offers money for our scalps. We'd be foolish to let you take ours."

"Will you two be watching over your chief?" McGurn asked.

The brave who'd been speaking nodded once.

"Then my guard can stand among you as he is. Will your chief be carrying a weapon?"

"He won't need one."

Unbuckling his gun belt and handing it to the brave, McGurn said, "Then neither will I. Is that acceptable?"

For a few seconds, the braves stared at McGurn and Clint without saying a word. Just when it seemed they might take a swing at the Army men and be done with it, the silent brave stepped forward to take the weapons from McGurn and the translator. "You two can go and talk. This one stays with us."

"Fine by me," Clint said as he kept his thumbs hooked over his gun belt.

Holding the flap of the tepee open, the brave waited until McGurn and the translator were inside before looking to Clint and snarling, "You make one move for that gun and I'll gut you like a freshly killed deer."

Clint nodded and stayed right where he was supposed to stand. Although he didn't say as much, he knew that if any of those warriors saw him reach for his gun, he'd have already lost the fight.

The tepee seemed smaller on the inside than it looked on the outside. Part of that was because of the design of the structure, which tapered to a point at the top, but most was due to the fact that there were five more braves already inside to form a wall behind the spot where Chief Tolfox sat. Tolfox motioned to some vacant ground around a small fire that was built in the middle of the area. McGurn and the translator both took their seats as Clint stood at the edge of the gathering. Without a word from either of the two braves that had escorted him in, a few more warriors took up positions next to and behind him. Clint knew that even his speed at drawing a pistol wouldn't do much good with that many eyes waiting for him to make a move.

"What did you bring me from Farelli?" Chief Tolfox asked.

McGurn blinked once and replied, "We bring you offerings of peace so we can end—"

"No," Tolfox snapped. "What did you bring?"

"I'm prepared to make an offer of trade, but this is only in the understanding that these attacks on our people will come to an end."

"What trade? How much?"

Although he kept his composure, McGurn was obviously

taken aback by the chief's straightforwardness. "Surely your people could use medicine or blankets."

"We have our own medicines and our women can make plenty of blankets."

"Then we can offer tools or maybe even some horses."

"That's better," Tolfox said with a grin.

McGurn's eyes narrowed as he took another look around the tepee. The braves held their positions and weren't brandishing their weapons. Although Clint had been surrounded, even he was allowed to watch over the talks as they'd agreed on outside. Therefore, McGurn's suspicious glare returned to Tolfox and stayed there.

"What would you propose, Chief?" McGurn asked.

The chief pulled in a breath and raised his chin. "One thousand dollars and the attacks will stop . . . for now."

"I came to discuss peace, not some temporary truce."

"A thousand now and another five thousand once we prove that we can uphold our end of this bargain. After that payment, you'll have your peace."

"This sounds more like a ransom," McGurn said.

Tolfox shrugged. "The only thing the white man understands is money. If you don't want to pay, we can come to another arrangement."

Finally, McGurn seemed pleased by what he'd heard. "There are plenty of arrangements to be made. Some can be beneficial to all of us. For example, I was thinking about a trade route between our two peoples that could help everyone equally."

Although McGurn had gathered a head of steam, Tolfox looked as if he'd bitten into a lemon. "If you don't have the cash, we'll accept horses or weapons. If you'd rather trade weapons, we might even be able to knock some off the agreed price."

"I wasn't aware this was about a price," McGurn said. "This is about settling whatever differences we have so that the attacks can stop."

"Your Blue Coats attack us, just as we attack you," Tolfox growled.

McGurn held up his hands and added, "The bloodshed must stop. We can come to an arrangement, but surely this wasn't just about getting us to pay you money."

Tolfox squinted and shook his head. "Where's Farelli? I should talk to him."

"Colonel Farelli has sent me to talk to you and I assure you I am authorized to make whatever arrangements are necessary."

Gritting his teeth in preparation for what looked to be a tirade, Tolfox snapped his head to one side when the sound of raised voices drifted in from outside. Just as the braves were getting nervous, the sounds from outside were joined by another.

A single rifle shot cracked through the air and punched a hole through the tepee.

NINETEEN

The second Clint heard the shot, he dropped to one knee and reached for his pistol. Another shot followed the first, but that was just different enough in pitch to have come from a different gun. Soon the camp outside was filled with gunshots. The inside of the tepee wasn't in much better condition.

One of the braves against the wall clutched his chest and dropped to his knees. His hands were slick with blood and his eyes were wide with blatant surprise. He tried to say something, but his words wouldn't come out. Then he fell over and the bullet wound could plainly be seen in his back.

"They're trying to kill me!" Tolfox shouted.

That was all the braves needed to hear before they swarmed in two directions. Half of the warriors closed in around the chief and the other half ran from the tepee. A few of them stayed right where they were, however. Those were the ones who'd surrounded Clint.

"I didn't fire a shot!" Clint said as one of the braves grabbed his arms and another drew a long blade from a scabbard hanging from his hip. "You were watching me the whole damn time!"

The Indian who'd laid down the law to Clint was the one who got up close to him now. Pressing the knife against Clint's throat, he said, "If any of those soldiers did this, you will die."

"We'll all have a better chance of surviving if we get the hell out of this tepee."

More shots were fired outside and a few of them tore through the tanned hide of the tepee. Two of the braves closest to Tolfox had grabbed hold of McGurn and the translator. While the translator seemed too petrified to move, McGurn had more of his wits about him. The lieutenant drove his elbow into the gut of the brave behind him, shoved another of the Indian warriors away, and dove for the spot where the ground met the tepee. There were stakes holding the hide in place, but McGurn was able to get outside with a bit of scrambling.

"Looks like your own men run away like dogs," the brave holding the knife on Clint said.

As more gunshots crackled outside, Clint waited for one to hit the tepee. When it did, the brave with the knife twitched, which was all the opening Clint needed. Clint's hand came up in a flicker of motion to knock the blade away from his throat. Before the brave could react, Clint drove his other fist into the Indian's stomach. The brave was made of solid muscle, but Clint's punch caused the Indian to stagger back half a step.

As much as Clint wanted to get out of that tepee, he couldn't just leave the translator sitting there. Clint rushed forward to scoop up the translator in one arm and keep running for the side of the tepee. Once the translator got his legs beneath him, he struggled to pull his own weight. Rather than wait for the smaller man to regain his balance, Clint tossed the translator into the tepee with enough force to pull the whole structure to one side.

Despite the impact of the translator's body against that side, the tepee remained upright. Clint turned to face the rest of the braves who now charged at him with weapons drawn. One of them caught a piece of lead that burned through the tepee and dropped to entangle the legs of a few others. There were more than enough to reach Clint, however, and the first one to get to him aimed a rifle at his face.

Clint drew his Colt and fired from the hip. His bullet drilled through the brave's hip and sent him spinning to the ground.

Another one of the Indians came at Clint with a knife. Clint was happy to let that one come forward until he was close enough to suit his purpose. At the last possible second, Clint snapped his gun arm upward so the side of his pistol cracked against the Indian's wrist, blocking the incoming knife moments before it was buried in Clint's chest. Clint twisted his upper body, allowed the blade to pass him by, and then pulled the knife out of the Indian's hand. The brave was strong, but Clint's blood was pumping fast enough to give him just enough extra steam to take the knife away. As soon as he had the knife, Clint slashed a large hole in the side of the tepee.

"Get out of here!" Clint shouted to the translator.

The translator cowered against the tepee, too scared to dive through the opening that was less than two feet away from him. Since there wasn't time to convince the translator to go, Clint placed his boot on the smaller man's shoulder and shoved him out. As soon as the translator was clear of the tepee, he found the strength to start running.

Clint took a step toward the rip himself, but was stopped by the Indian whose knife had been taken away. Turning to swing at the brave, Clint felt his Colt bounce off the large Indian. Although he could have made certain the warrior wouldn't follow him or anyone ever again, Clint decided to put all of his efforts into just getting out of the tepee.

More shots were coming from the other end of camp. Now that he was outside, Clint could make out some voices as well. Several of them must have come from the Indians, but one of them stood out from the rest.

"It's all over, dammit! The deal's off!"

It was Nolan. Not only was he screaming at the top of his lungs, but he was also firing his rifle at the tepee. Clint saw the gunman firing and working the lever of his rifle to alternate between firing at the tepee and shooting at the Indians who tried to bring him down.

"What the hell are you doing, Nolan?" Clint shouted as he ran around the tepee. He kept his head low to avoid an incoming shot, but wasn't so concerned when he saw the crazed look in Nolan's eyes.

Nolan's coat was open so he could get to almost every gun at his disposal. After firing one more shot into a nearby Indian, he wrapped both hands around the stock and swung the rifle into the head of another. Then Nolan drew both pistols from his double-rig holster and shouted, "The cavalry's comin'! Bring them outta there, Adams! The cavalry's comin'!"

The translator put his back to the entire camp and ran for the surrounding rocks.

The scout was nowhere to be found.

Before Clint could try to make sense of what was happening, he heard McGurn's booming voice over the chaos.

"Stand down!" McGurn shouted. "That's an—" was all he could get out before a bullet was fired into his chest.

McGurn staggered and dropped to one knee.

Clint ran toward the lieutenant as Nolan kept on screaming.

"The lieutenant's dead!" Nolan hollered. "Someone spread the word these savages killed an Army officer!"

Just then, Tolfox emerged from the tepee surrounded by his braves. As soon as he laid eyes upon the chief, Nolan ran forward and pointed both guns at Tolfox. "It's all over!" Nolan announced. "You're—"

Clint's modified Colt barked once and sent a bullet

through Nolan's skull. Nolan's fingers clenched around his triggers, but he was already falling to the ground and sent both shots straight into the dirt.

"Done!" Clint said as he quickly pointed his pistol to the sky. "I don't know what started this, but it's done! Everybody just calm down before anyone else gets hurt."

There was a rustling behind Clint, but before he could do anything about it he felt a sharp pain at the back of his head. A single thump filled Clint's ears, blackness filled his eyes, and his legs turned into limp noodles beneath the rest of him.

TWENTY

Clint opened his eyes and immediately regretted it.

The first thing he felt was enough pain from the back of his head to convince him his skull had been cracked. The only way to make it hurt any worse was to move, which he tried to do out of pure reflex. Thankfully he couldn't move more than an inch or so in any direction before he was stopped.

He couldn't see anything, but it took a few more seconds for Clint to realize there was something tied over his eyes. Then he felt the first pain again as his blindfold dug into the sore spot on his head. After a bit of squirming, Clint figured out he was lying on his side. Since the pain was only getting worse, he decided to sit still for a second and let his ears do some of the work.

It was fairly quiet wherever he was. Apart from a few birds and some running water, the only things Clint could hear were some subdued voices. The couple of words he could pick out weren't English. While Clint might not have been an expert in languages, he recognized Navajo when he heard it. That bit of knowledge caused a whole flood of thoughts to cut loose within his head. Even those hurt.

Trying to keep his movements subtle, Clint flexed the

muscles in his arms and legs. Sure enough, those were all tied up pretty well. From the feel of the surfaces against his hands, Clint knew he was lying on the ground. There were fires crackling in the distance and a couple of subdued conversations being held. That was fairly encouraging.

Clint didn't need to feel around his waist to guess his weapons were missing. In the end, he had to take comfort from the simple fact that he was still breathing. When he thought back to what had happened before he was knocked out, Clint had to wonder how that little miracle had occurred.

When Clint tried to stretch his back, he heard a flutter of whispers coming from only a few feet away. He froze and strained his ears to try and pick up anything at all. The only word he thought he heard was Navajo for "awake."

Because his hands were tied and he didn't have any weapons, Clint didn't have many options. Since his feet were also tied and he couldn't sit upright or even get a look at where he was, his options dwindled down to something close to none. Rather than count on another miracle taking place, he kept motionless and tried to act like he was still asleep.

Clint could feel someone coming closer. The sound of movement was a subtle brushing nearby, followed by a vague heat that could only come from another body. Soon Clint felt something soft brushing against his arm. That was followed by the same voice that had been talking a few moments ago. The voice was most definitely female.

"Are you awake?" she asked.

There was silence before Clint felt a hand brush against his cheek. After that, light flooded into his eyes in such a rush that he was blinded for a few seconds. Peeling open his eyelids felt more like tearing them apart after they'd been sewn shut.

After a few blinks, Clint could make out some details. There was a woman with smooth, dark skin looking at him.

One thing was for certain: it was too late to pretend to be asleep. Clint lifted his head to look back at her. When he tried to ask a question, he realized something was still wrapped around the lower portion of his face. The woman glanced about nervously before slowly reaching out to pull the gag away from his mouth.

Stopping short of removing the gag, she warned, "You will have to stay quiet."

As much as it hurt to do so, Clint nodded.

The woman had a slender face that was accentuated by soft, high cheekbones. Her skin was the color of desert clay and her hair had the thick, lustrous shine of a full-blooded native. She was careful while removing the gag and watched Clint's face every second of the way. When she peeled back the gag, she winced as if she feared some sort of punishment might come from any direction. Leaning down, she placed her lips so close to him that Clint could feel the heat from her breath when she spoke.

"Ahiga is still very angry," she said. "It is best if you stay asleep for a while longer."

"But where—"

Before Clint could get another word out, he felt the woman press down on top of him as if she were trying to gently smother him. It was a strange combination as she tried to keep him from making another sound without actually hurting him. Since she didn't want to take her hands away from the gag, Clint tried again to speak while he still could. Suddenly, something pressed against his mouth.

Since her own face was closer to him than her hands, she quickly placed her lips against his mouth. Even after Clint stopped trying to talk, it took her a few seconds to let up on the pressure. Her lips were warm and dry and her eyelids fluttered as if even she couldn't believe she was kissing him. After a few more seconds, she moved her head back just enough for her to speak.

"I've been watching you since those soldiers rode into

camp," she said. "I know you were not working with the killer who started all the shooting. You must trust me and keep quiet."

"How long?" Clint asked.

"I'll come for you again." With that, she eased the gag up over Clint's mouth. She had some trouble getting it in place, since he squirmed and twisted his head to fight her. When she finally pulled the gag down in frustration, she stared at him with urgency. "You must stay quiet."

"Just tell me your name," Clint insisted.

Sighing in frustration and looking around, she met his eyes once more and said, "My name is Fawn."

Rather than say anything else, Clint nodded and allowed the gag to be placed over his mouth. Fawn also put the blindfold on again, but made sure it was loose enough for Clint to see some light at the edges of the cloth. He closed his eyes and tried to relax. He needed the rest anyway.

TWENTY-ONE

Clint actually managed to fall asleep a few times. With the pain in his head still throbbing, he figured at least one of those times had actually been him passing out. Even so, he felt his strength slowly leaking back the more rest he tried to get. Just getting that one glimpse at his surroundings and being able to see a bit of daylight did him a world of good.

He could hear voices nearby, and every now and then, heavy footsteps would approach Clint and then stomp away. One of those times, Clint heard someone mention Ahiga by name. By the sound of it, Fawn had been right. Whoever Ahiga was, he was definitely angry. The few words Clint could catch and understand were not encouraging.

As near as Clint could tell, Ahiga wanted to kill him. One or two of the times he'd approached had probably been for that very purpose. Since he couldn't move, didn't have any weapons, and didn't even know where he was, Clint did the only thing he could do. He kept still and pretended to be asleep. Despite the fact that it took no effort for him to lie there, Clint felt like it was the hardest path he could have chosen.

Every time he felt those stomping footsteps, Clint wanted to jump up and see who was making them.

Whenever he heard threats being hurled at his back, Clint wanted to sit up and answer them.

But he didn't do any of those things. He gritted his teeth and played dead until he thought he'd rather take his chances with facing real death before rolling over one more time. Fortunately, the next set of footsteps he heard weren't angry. They were more like soft cat's feet padding upon the floor. Once those steps got close to him, Clint heard a familiar voice.

"Are you awake?" Fawn whispered.

Clint nodded.

Her hands brushed against his face to remove the blindfold and gag with soft precision. Clint opened his eyes and only needed a second or two to adjust to the dim glow coming in from outside. His throat was dry, so he spoke softly to keep from hacking loud enough to draw attention.

"Where . . . am I?" he croaked.

"Here," Fawn said as she slipped an arm beneath Clint's shoulder and helped him to sit up. Once he was situated, she held a waterskin to his mouth.

The water was cool, but still burned when it trickled over his parched throat. A few more sips were enough to remedy the situation and soon Clint was gulping the water down.

"You're in our camp," Fawn said before Clint could ask his question again. "It's about half a day's ride from the spot where those soldiers were killed."

"They're all dead?"

She blinked and lowered her head. Her raven black hair drifted down to frame the long, smooth lines of her face and swayed like strands of silk in a gentle breeze. "The leader was killed and . . . you killed the other one."

Hearing that put a knot in Clint's stomach. "The other one . . . did he kill many others?"

"Four," Fawn replied. "Including one of your own. Our medicine man is singing for two more, but they are hurt very badly."

"Nolan killed the lieutenant?" Clint said under his breath. Seeing the puzzled expression on Fawn's face, he asked, "Did the one who started shooting kill the leader of the soldiers?"

She slowly shook her head. "I don't know. Ahiga says that one killed another soldier that was found a little ways outside the other camp."

Clint figured she was talking about the scout that had brought McGurn to the meeting. He didn't know why Nolan would kill that scout, but Clint also didn't know why the gunman would just open fire the way he did. One thing he did know was that he intended to find out.

"Can you untie my hands?" Clint asked.

Although she seemed reluctant, Fawn didn't refuse him right away. "Now is not a good time for you to leave."

"Ahiga wants to kill me. If I don't leave soon, I'll be dead." Clint could tell his words were having an impact, but it wasn't a big enough impact just yet. "Why did you help me?" he asked.

Fawn blinked and nervously shifted her eyes away from him. "I was there when the shooting started. I saw what you tried to do."

"I didn't want that to happen," Clint insisted.

"I know. If you hadn't stopped that killer, there would have been a lot more blood spilled. If Ahiga makes his voice heard by enough of our people, blood will be spilled anyway."

"Then let me go. Nobody will know what you did. They'll just think I escaped on my own. You came this far, Fawn. Just do what you know is right."

"You'll go to the rest of the soldiers and bring them here," she said. "I cannot allow that."

"Then why come to me at all?"

Since she seemed to have trouble finding the right words, Fawn kept her face close to him and her eyes locked upon Clint's. He seized the opportunity to lean forward a bit more until he felt his lips touch hers. The moment Clint started the kiss, Fawn had no trouble finishing it. She slipped both hands up to slide against Clint's face and slip around through his hair. All Clint had to do was push forward just a little bit more and she parted her lips to let his tongue slip into her mouth. She returned the favor and tasted him as if she'd been starving for weeks and was now finally getting the feast she'd been after.

Before long, Clint felt her body pressing against him and her hands wandering over his shoulders until they caressed the muscles in his arms. When she slid her hand down along his stomach and then reached a little lower, Fawn touched the erection growing between Clint's legs.

"If you're not going to let me go," Clint said, "then you must have come here for a reason."

Fawn locked her eyes upon Clint, straddled him, and then slowly peeled her tunic up and over her head.

TWENTY-TWO

Fawn moved with as much grace as her namesake. She wriggled out of her tunic and set it aside without making a sound. She then started to pull apart the buttons of Clint's shirt, but only loosened enough for her to slide her hands under his clothing to touch the bare skin of his chest. When she leaned her head down to close the distance between herself and Clint, she closed her eyes and waited for his touch.

She didn't have to wait long. Clint leaned up to kiss her, savoring the feel of her lips as her hands continued to move over his skin. Rather than think about the death and blood and pain that filled his more recent memories, Clint gave in to what was happening. If he was to be executed by these Indians, he wasn't about to turn his nose up at one last chance for something as pleasant as Fawn's soft body on top of him.

Fawn never took her lips off him as she unfastened Clint's belt and then pulled open the front of his jeans. Sliding her entire body down a little ways, she eased his pants down and then guided him between her legs. Even Fawn's hands were soft and smooth as she stroked Clint's rigid cock a few times before easing it inside of her. When she lowered herself down onto him, Fawn let out a contented breath and closed her eyes as if she were in the middle of a dream.

Come to think of it, Clint wondered if he was the one dreaming. As Fawn rocked slowly on top of him, the rest of the world seemed to quiet down. When he turned his head to get a look on either side of her, all he could see were thick shadows. The only indication he had of the outside world was the warm breeze that drifted in.

Fawn straightened her back and placed her hands upon Clint's chest. Gazing down at him, she let her head droop forward so her hair spilled over her shoulders to brush against his neck and chest. Her fingertips pressed into his skin as she slowly ground her hips back and forth. Just as she'd rocked all the way forward, she pushed her hips a bit more to take every last inch of him inside of her. She clenched her eyes shut and tensed as a little quiver worked its way through her body.

More than anything, Clint wanted to get his hands on her. He strained against the ropes that were binding him just so he could cup her backside in both hands and guide her so he could pump into her. At the moment, he wanted that even more than to get away from wherever it was he was being held. Perhaps that was written on his face, because Fawn let her body drop forward so she could reach behind him and grab on to his bindings.

Instead of untying him, she gripped the ropes around his wrists and rested her head close to Clint's face. "I will let you go," she whispered. "I just wanted to keep you here for a little longer."

"I'm . . . glad you did," Clint replied as he was nearly overwhelmed by the combined sensations of Fawn's hard little nipples brushing against his chest and her pussy tightening around him.

"I saw the fire in your eyes when you first rode into camp," she continued. "I could not stop thinking about it."

Clint leaned back and pumped up into her. The move took Fawn by surprise, but the look in her eyes showed it was a pleasant one. She started to speak again, but her breath was taken away as Clint pumped into her again.

His hips thrust up like a piston, filling Fawn's body until the little climax that had already started to fade became something that filled her entire body like an explosion. She pulled in a breath, which became a gasp, and then bit down on her lower lip to keep from crying out.

Clint's hands were balled into fists behind him. He lowered his hips to discover that Fawn had gotten her legs beneath herself and was squatting on top of him. She lowered her hips to follow his every move. The moment she seemed to catch her breath, Clint pumped into her and took it away again.

Fawn's climax made every muscle in her body tense. Her fingers dug into his skin and she snapped her head back until the pleasure finally subsided enough for her to open her eyes again. Sweat glistened from her brow as she pumped her hips faster and faster in short strokes that sent Clint directly over his own threshold.

When he exploded inside of her, it was so intense that he thought he might have snapped his hands free of the ropes. But the knots of those ropes had already been untied. Fawn remained on top of him and gently placed a finger upon his lips.

By the time he caught his own breath, Clint felt the bit of weight that had been on top of him move away. He brought his arms around to work a few of the kinks from his shoulders and asked, "Why help me?"

"You tried to help before. You should not be killed for that."

"And . . . the rest?"

She crawled next to him, a smooth, naked presence in the shadows. "That was because I wanted to. Now go."

Clint was never one to refuse a lady.

TWENTY-THREE

Clint leaned forward to untie the ropes around his ankles. He also needed to pull up his jeans if he wanted to stand up. By the time he was done with those things, Fawn had slipped back into her tunic and was gone. He could still smell the natural scent of her hair and skin. He could still taste her upon his tongue, but had to force those things from his mind as he crept in the darkness to get his bearings.

It didn't take much creeping for him to figure out he was in the back of a wagon. Now that he was no longer blindfolded, he could see the size of the space he was in. And now that he could move on his own, he could feel the boards creak beneath him. The boards didn't move very much, however, which didn't quite fit with the idea of being in a wagon. Clint figured out that last part the moment he carefully stuck his head out the back of the wagon, which was covered by a set of tanned hides.

The wagon didn't have any wheels. The axles were still in place, but the body of the wagon was sitting upon the ground like a small hut. Clint couldn't make out the entire camp from where he was, but he could see a few other wagons situated directly upon the ground in a similar manner.

Judging by the condition of those wagons, they could have been scavenged from some of the recent attacks.

There was another wagon a few paces away from Clint and a few more on the opposite end of the camp. A fire was built in the middle of everything else like the hub of a wheel. Two tepees were set up on the other end of the camp as well and it seemed that most of the people in the camp were focusing on the largest of them.

A few bare-chested men in war paint sat near the fire, but they were watching the largest tepee as well. Since none of the Indians in the camp spared a look in Clint's direction, the others either didn't know he was there or figured he wasn't about to be going anywhere. Considering how well he'd been restrained, it was no wonder they didn't give him much thought. Clint's head was pounding again and his legs were wobbly beneath him. If it hadn't been for Fawn's help, he wouldn't have made it out.

Just then, a large man stepped out from one of the broken wagons. He pushed aside the hide covering at the back of the wagon and stood up to an impressive height. Even in the shadows, his scowl was plain to see. Clint pulled his head back inside the moment he saw the big Indian shift his attention toward him. Using the tip of his finger, Clint pulled aside another edge of the door's covering to get a look outside.

The big Indian must have only glanced toward Clint's wagon, because he was already moving along to the large tepee. It seemed the other Indians were just as rattled to have the giant looking at them because their heads were bowed like the lesser members of a wolf pack.

Waiting until everyone in sight was looking away, Clint slipped out of the wagon and ducked around the battered wooden structure. There was no doubt the wagon was left over from one of the attacks. The planks Clint brushed against were scorched and chipped in several places. He even found a few bullet holes as he ran his hands along the wood to make sure he didn't accidentally step away from cover.

With his back to the wagon and the rest of the camp, Clint could look out onto a wide-open stretch of rocky land. The sun was down and the stars were scattered across a clear, inky sky. There was even half a moon out to cast some pale light onto the ground, making the prospect of running for his life seem awfully inviting. But he knew he might not have to run.

He'd dealt with Indians several times. Clint had even dealt with the Navajo more than once. He knew the tribes were just like any other group of human beings. Some were good and some were bad. He knew this tribe was on the warpath. But no matter what tribe they were or what they were up to, every Indian knew the value of a good horse.

Eclipse wasn't just a good horse. He was one of the best things to walk on four legs. There wasn't a man in his right mind who would leave a horse like that behind.

Rather than go running into the night like some kind of fool, Clint kept sneaking around the edge of the camp until he could hear the combined shifting of a couple dozen hooves. That sound, along with several deep, snuffing breaths, told him he was getting close to the spot where the Indians were corralling their livestock.

Clint wasn't exactly feeling his best, but he forced himself to crouch down low and move quietly. Every one of his joints ached and his head felt like it was about to pop like a tick, but he managed to get close enough to see the makeshift corral.

The horses were being guarded by two Indians carrying rifles. They sat on either end of the horses, which were tied to a row of posts that had been driven into the ground. Clint could tell the members of the tribe valued their horses very much, since they kept the corral so close to the central tepees. That sliver of knowledge wasn't an even trade for the inconvenience that the location posed.

If Eclipse was anywhere nearby, he'd be in that corral. And if Clint was going to get into that corral, he was going to have to get a lot closer to most of the armed braves in the camp. It wasn't an inviting prospect, but there weren't many better ones.

Before he could go much farther, Clint saw one of the Indians that had been sitting by the fire stand up and walk toward the wagon where Clint had been held.

Just when Clint was thinking his escape would have to be sped up a bit more, he saw another figure rush toward the fire to step directly in front of the inquisitive Indian. It was Fawn. She spoke a few hurried words to the other man and got him to walk back to the fire. After that, nobody else seemed too interested in checking on Clint's whereabouts.

TWENTY-FOUR

Clint made it all the way to the makeshift corral without much trouble. He got close enough to see that Eclipse was there and appeared to be unharmed. Just to be certain, Clint made his presence known to the Darley Arabian. The stallion's ears pricked up and he started walking toward Clint's outstretched hand. Rather than make Eclipse move too much, Clint met him halfway.

"You ready for a run, boy?" he whispered as he gave the stallion a quick once-over.

Eclipse strained against his tether but kept from tugging too hard on the post.

Clint's saddle was gone, but that didn't bother him as much as the emptiness he felt at his hip where his holster should have been. His life had been saved by that gun more times than he could count. Even though he could put some work into another pistol, Clint felt confident that he had a better-than-average chance of getting his own gun back.

There were a good number of Indians in the camp, but most of them seemed to be in or around the largest tepee. Clint spotted a few armed men outside the tepee, the ones by the fire, and a few random others milling about one of the broken wagons. With a little bit of scouting, Clint thought he could see where the Indians kept their weapons. At the very least, he'd also be able to get a good idea of the number of braves in that camp so he could have something definite to report when he made it back to Fort Winstead.

With so much activity in the large tepee, the guards outside of that spot had their eyes mostly focused away from it. They cast their eyes about to look for intruders or watched a few of the nearby squaws. Fawn seemed to be doing her part as far as that was concerned, and she kept at least two of the men occupied with small talk or the occasional smile.

Ironically enough, the safest route for Clint to take at the moment was directly around the back of the large tepee. There was only one man posted back there, but he sat on the ground cross-legged, staring away from the camp with at least two yards between himself and the tepee. With all the talking and scuffling coming from within the tepee, Clint figured he could sneak directly behind the man without him knowing.

As Clint made his approach, he got to within a few feet of the lone guard without causing so much as a curious twitch in the other man. Since his luck seemed to be holding out, Clint figured he might as well find out where his gun was from someone who might actually know. He ignored the pain in his head and nearly every other part of his body as he crept up behind the lone Indian. Timing his steps to the rise and fall of voices from the nearby tepee, Clint made it to a spot directly behind the Indian.

Just as the Indian was shifting in his spot, Clint reached out to place one hand over the Indian's mouth and the other arm around the Indian's neck.

"Don't make a sound or I'll snap your neck," Clint hissed into the Indian's ear.

The Indian struggled and kicked, but his limbs were already losing steam as Clint put more pressure on his windpipe. He grabbed at Clint's head, but Clint simply leaned his head back and switched it to the other side of the Indian's skull. By the time the Indian tried to pull Clint's hands away, his movements were already too weak to get the job done.

Cinching in his grip a bit tighter, Clint whispered, "If you understand me, just nod."

The Indian kept pulling at Clint's arm and kicking at the ground.

"Fine, then," Clint said. "I guess I'll just kill you."

Not only did the Indian stop struggling, but he also nodded as quickly as he could, considering his current predicament.

"Good. That's what I thought." Easing up on the pressure, Clint gave the Indian enough room to breathe, but not nearly enough to get free. "Where do you keep the weapons that were taken from your prisoners?"

"We don't . . . take prisoners."

"You took me," Clint growled as he once again tightened his grip around the Indian's neck. "Where's my gun?"

"Ahiga . . . he took it. He carries it now."

"And where's Ahiga?"

"In the . . . council," the Indian replied as he knocked his head back against Clint. "The council being held there."

Clint reflexively looked at the tepee behind him. Judging by the hushed voices from inside, most of the people were listening while one man was doing the majority of the talking. If Clint sat still and paid attention, he'd be able to make out what was being said. For the moment, he had plenty on his plate.

"Are you the only man guarding this spot?" Clint asked. It took a moment for the Indian to answer, so Clint tensed the muscles in his arm before the other man could think too long about it.

"Yes," the Indian snapped. "Your Army doesn't know about this place."

Clint nodded. "That's better. Now sleep tight."

TWENTY-FIVE

The Indian guard lay on his side next to Clint. It hadn't taken much more pressure to put the man down, but Clint had made certain to wait until the man had stopped moving for a bit before letting go of his neck. Clint didn't know exactly how much time he'd have until the guard woke up, but he figured he could at least stay put long enough to listen to what was being said inside the tepee. Keeping one hand on the unconscious Indian's arm so he'd know when the man stirred, Clint kept his ears focused on the council meeting and his eyes open for any sign that he might be discovered.

Most of the talking inside the tepee seemed to come from one man who had a weathered, aged voice. After a few sentences, Clint knew enough to be certain this wasn't Chief Tolfox. Apart from the tone of the man's voice, one thing that struck Clint was the fact that most of the men spoke English.

"We have heard these promises before," the old man said, "and your words have only led to blood being spilled."

"My promises have paid off," another man replied. This one Clint recognized as Tolfox. "My actions have put money in your pockets and allowed your tribe to flourish."

"We must live in our way. The white men can kill each other for money. We take what we need from our land."

"And your land is being cut away!" Tolfox said. "You can talk all you want about the white man's money, but that's the currency of this land! It may not have been that way before, but that's how it is right now. Any one of you who disagrees with me can say so!"

There was a quiet pause and a few grumblings, but Clint didn't hear anyone speak up against what Tolfox had said. In fact, when Tolfox continued, Clint could imagine the smug grin that would go along with the tone in his voice.

"I see these people agree with me," Tolfox said. "Perhaps it is time for them to accept their true leader."

Unlike the previous statement, that one sure got a noisy response. Several voices flared up, but one of them stood out from the rest. It was a deep, bellowing voice that sounded like something closer to thunder. "You may pose as our chief to the white man," the thundering voice warned, "but do not try to take that place here."

Clint couldn't see what was going on inside the tepee, but he could feel the tension as if it were something that seeped outside through the hide wall and wooden posts.

Several people spoke in Navajo. A few even spoke in a different Indian tongue, but soon they were all quieted.

"Enough blood has already been shed, Ahiga," the old man said. "We speak in council to keep from spilling any more."

"And he makes us speak in the white man's tongue," Ahiga growled.

Tolfox immediately replied. "I'd be happy to discuss matters in my own language if you'd prefer."

"You are among our people!" Ahiga said. "You are speaking to our chief! You should speak using our words!"

"We speak about the white man," the old man interrupted. "We speak about the white man's money and the white man's Army intruding on our land, so we will speak in the white man's tongue. We do not have the time to find another plot of neutral ground."

There was a bit more grumbling, followed by some calming breaths. Those things were enough for Clint to feel a lessening of the tension that had been so thick in the air a few moments ago.

"This is the last time we try to deal with this man," the old man announced.

Clint thought the old man might have been referring to Tolfox, but Tolfox's was among the voices who agreed to what the old man had said.

"In the past, he has at least kept his word," the old man continued. "This time ends with death."

"It hasn't ended yet," Ahiga said. "It will end with death, but that death will be Farelli's."

"Was he there when this last blood was spilled?"

"No. He must have known what was going to happen, which is why he made certain not to be anywhere near us."

"What do you say to this?" the old man asked.

Tolfox was the one to reply. "This could be true. Farelli speaks with a forked tongue. We have always known this, but he never had the spine to try something as bold as this."

"He does not respect us," Ahiga growled. "He cheats and lies like every other white man."

Ignoring Ahiga's words, Tolfox said, "Farelli meant to cheat us, but I don't know about the man he sent in his place. That one seemed to be true when he spoke. Some of his men seemed true as well."

"And what of the man that was taken?" the old man asked. "Did he know or was he one of the liars?"

"We'll find out as soon as he is awake," Ahiga replied. "Fawn tells me he was hurt and has not opened his eyes."

"But . . . he lives?" the old man asked.

"Yes. He lives."

When Tolfox spoke this time, there was more venom in his tone than all the other times combined. "If these men lie, why should we listen to this one? If he is who I think he is . . ."

"Who is he?" Ahiga asked. "Tell us."

"I think he is a hired gunfighter. He was probably brought to kill us."

"From what I have been told, he would have had his chance to kill if he'd wanted that," the old man pointed out. "My word stands. He is not to be hurt until we learn more about him."

"And what if he does not talk to you?" Tolfox asked.

"Then we will set him free."

"And abandon our home?"

"Home?" Ahiga bellowed among plenty of other rumbling from others within the tepee. "We sleep within these crippled wagons and you call it a home? You are no better than the Army! At least they give us some other patch of land to make our home."

"You want to eat the scraps the Army feeds to you?" Tolfox asked.

The old man quickly jumped in. "We will not fight among ourselves." From the pained grunts and groans Clint could hear, it sounded as if the old man was straining to move or get to his feet. "Our dealing with your friend Farelli is over. We do not need his money, and the lands he promised us are already about to be taken away."

"He has kept our tribes from coming to harm," Tolfox added.

"No," the old man snapped. "He has kept *your* tribe from being harmed. Ours gets barren land and empty words."

"He has paid us both handsomely."

"This time he has only paid in blood. It is the last time. Go now, back to your land, and do not come back again."

Tolfox was quick to say, "But our tribes have—"

"You have a greedy heart and a trickster's tongue," the old man said. "Now we have all seen the trouble you bring.

If the Crow wish to deal with us, let them send another to speak for them. Ahiga, talk to the man who sleeps and see what he knows about Farelli's lies. If he doesn't know, be sure to tell him. It is best for us all to know the tricksters among us. I am tired, so I must sleep."

The old man spoke some words in Navajo. Clint picked out just enough to know he was asking for someone to help him get to his bed.

"But there is more we can do!" Tolfox protested.

"No!" Ahiga growled. "We are through. Go. Now."

Clint followed that advice as well.

TWENTY-SIX

"Stand aside, woman!" Ahiga said. He was a tall Navajo with hair that hung straight down past his shoulders to frame a face that looked like an angry mask carved into stone. He wore beaded bands around his upper arms that had markings matching the ones stitched into the scabbard he wore around his waist. Although he'd grabbed hold of Fawn's shoulders, Ahiga only used enough force to move her to one side.

Fawn struggled to maintain her ground, even though it was obviously a losing battle. However, she was able to block half of the door to the grounded wagon with her arm and one leg. "No. You'll hurt him."

"What does that matter to you?"

She paused for a second and then thought of something that brought a relieved smile to her face. "Our chief has said that he should not be harmed."

"I know what he said. Now step aside."

Having run out of things to say, Fawn lowered her eyes and shuffled the rest of the way from the wagon.

Ahiga had one hand upon the flap at the back of the wagon, but stopped before stepping inside. "I saw the way you looked at him," he told her. "You tended to him as if he was your own."

She shrugged, neither confirming nor denying what he said. Judging by the assurance etched into every last one of Ahiga's features, he wouldn't have been swayed by much of anything anyway.

He shook his head slowly, pulled the flap open, and stepped inside.

Fawn closed her eyes and clenched her hands into small fists. Her muscles tensed as if she were ready to run, but her brow was furrowed with the knowledge that there was nowhere she could go. Fortunately, she didn't have to wait long for the inevitable storm.

"Fawn!" Ahiga bellowed. "What is the meaning of this?"

She waited silently in her spot.

When Ahiga stuck his head out of the wagon, he asked, "Did you know about this?"

"Know about what?" she asked in a timid voice.

Ahiga reached out with one hand to grab hold of Fawn's wrist so he could pull her into the wagon. Not only did she need to move her feet quickly to keep from falling on her face, but she needed to duck her head in time to keep from smacking it against the side of the wagon. As soon as she was inside, she felt Ahiga's other hand clamp around the back of her neck.

Allowing herself to be pulled further inside like a dog that was about to get its nose pushed into its own mess, Fawn was pointed toward the back of the wagon.

"This," Ahiga said. "Did you know about this?"

Fawn looked up to find a genuine surprise. Clint was sitting with his back against the wagon and his legs casually splayed in front of him. In fact, he even waved when he saw he had both of the others' attention.

"No . . . I . . . I didn't think . . ." Fawn stammered.

Keeping one hand on Fawn's neck, Ahiga drew the long blade from the scabbard at his side and held it toward Clint. "That's right. You didn't think," he said to her as he shoved Fawn back outside. "Bring another man here, and not one of the fools that was supposed to be guarding this one!"

Clint was glad he'd managed to surprise Fawn so completely. That way he got a response from her that was so genuine it probably helped keep both of them healthy for a while longer. The instant he started to move, Clint saw the big Indian lunge toward him another few inches until the edge of the blade was almost close enough to draw blood.

Shifting away from the tribal language he'd used with Fawn, Ahiga spoke to Clint in clear, very angry English. "If you want to live, white man, you will stay right where you are."

"And if I'd wanted to escape," Clint replied, "I would've been long gone already."

Ahiga wasn't exactly chuckling at Clint's comment, but he obviously saw the sense in it. He lowered his blade, but kept it where he could sink it into Clint's chest easily enough if the occasion called for it. "I've got some questions for you, white man," Ahiga said.

Clint nodded. "And I can think of one or two for you, as well."

TWENTY-SEVEN

Clint allowed himself to be tied up again before meeting with anyone. Compared to the knots that had been holding him back before, the few that Ahiga tied weren't too bad. A rope was lashed around Clint's wrists and tied tightly, but his feet were left free so he could leave the wagon and be led to the large tepee near the middle of the camp.

Ahiga shoved Clint roughly in front of him, making sure the blade in his hand could always be felt against the small of Clint's back. Seeing the questioning glances of the other men in camp, Ahiga would give Clint another push or tighten his grip upon his knife to make sure it was obvious who was in charge.

After being shoved into the tepee, Clint was practically knocked onto his knees and forced to the ground. It took a bit of work, but Clint got his legs untangled so he was sitting with them crossed and his hands resting on his lap.

The old man sat on a woven mat near the center of the tepee. He was dressed in weathered skins and held a wooden staff carved with intricate markings and decorated with beaded leather straps and bright feathers. His face was calm and had more lines etched into it than the desert floor. He watched Clint the way he might watch a shadow crawl across the ground. His eyes were sharp and his mouth was curled into a subtle smile.

Before the old man could say anything, Clint met his eyes and spoke a simple Navajo greeting.

"You know our language?" the old man asked.

"Just enough to keep me out of trouble," Clint replied.

The old man smiled a bit wider. "That remains to be seen."

"I suppose it does."

After a few seconds, the old man said, "My people call me Mingan."

Clint thought about that for a few seconds and asked, "Gray Wolf?"

The old man nodded once. "Since I am the eldest and have spoken the most as to where we should go, some have also called me Chief."

"I'm sure you've earned it."

"Do not speak when you do not know."

"I've known more than a few Navajo," Clint explained. "They don't strike me as the sort who follow anyone and call someone Chief just because they're old."

Ahiga knocked Clint's shoulder with his arm and growled, "Watch your tongue, white man."

Mingan raised one hand, which was enough to pull back Ahiga's reins. "He is right. I am old and my people do not follow just anyone. They have been making mistakes of late."

Clint nodded. "If you're talking about what happened when that fool started shooting, I don't know what that was or whose mistake was to blame."

"He drew his guns and started shooting," one of the other Indians in the tepee said. "I was there! He was crazy!"

Silencing the other man with the same hand he'd used to silence Ahiga, Mingan asked, "What is your name?"

"Clint Adams."

"Why did that crazy man start shooting, Clint Adams?"

"First of all, you can just call me Clint. Secondly, I don't know why he started shooting."

"You rode to the meeting with him," Mingan pointed out. "He must have spoken of something during that ride."

"He sure as hell didn't speak about shooting up the place before anyone could do what we were there to do. And before you ask, I'll tell you we were there to talk peace. Lieutenant McGurn wanted to put an end to the attacks your people were making and he wanted to do it without having to kill any of those people in the process."

Narrowing his eyes, Mingan asked, "Do you know why those attacks were made?"

"From what I've seen, it looks like you've got some problems with the Army." Choosing his next words carefully, Clint added, "And I've heard there may be a problem with a certain Army colonel."

By the look on Mingan's face, he suspected something but he didn't pursue it just then. "You know Colonel Farelli?"

"Yes I do."

"What has he told you of us?"

"Not much more than what I've seen with my own eyes. Your tribe is attacking unarmed wagons and killing soldiers. Whatever your reasons may be, you've got to know that's not a good way to go about things. Whatever you're trying to—"

"My tribe," Mingan interrupted, "is cut into pieces. What you see here is only part of a tribe. We are more like pebbles that have all drifted to the bottom of the same lake. We are together for now, but we belong to a greater whole, which is far away from here."

"Where's the rest of your tribe?" Clint asked.

"Most of us are Navajo, but we have banded together after being herded to reservations or slaughtered like cattle. We come together now to try and collect something we can all take back to our people."

"Collect what?"

Ahiga slammed his fist against the ground with enough force to make Clint jump. "Enough of your questions," he growled. "You were brought here to answer, not ask!"

Mingan nodded. "He is right. I need to know what your Army plans to do next."

"It's not my Army. I was just along to help things go smoother."

While Ahiga chuckled, Mingan said, "I have heard you killed your own partner to stop him from harming more of my people."

Clint winced at that. Even though he knew well enough what he'd done, it stung to hear it put so bluntly. "He wasn't my partner and I don't know what the hell he was doing. As far as I'm concerned, he was lighting a fire that would have burned down me and everyone else at that meeting."

"Well said," Mingan replied. "What you did . . . the way you stopped that man . . . it tells me that you are speaking the truth about not knowing what he meant to do. So spilling blood was not the intention of your Army officer?"

Shaking his head, Clint said, "I know Lieutenant McGurn well enough to know he wouldn't take part in turning a peaceful talk into a slaughter."

Mingan looked over to Ahiga. The bigger Indian winced in a way similar to how Clint had winced moments ago. For Ahiga, however, the sting seemed to come from admitting that Clint was right. The big Indian nodded and said, "The lieutenant spoke words of peace and he never drew a weapon against us." Shifting his eyes to Clint, he added, "But the crazy man with the guns was shooting at the tent, trying to kill the officer as well as Tolfox."

"Is this true?" Mingan asked.

"Who is Tolfox?" Clint asked.

"Answer the question, white man," Ahiga warned.

As much as Clint wanted to say whatever the Indians

wanted to hear, he simply wasn't about to gamble on the fact that he could get anything past the crystal-clear eyes in the old man's head. Finally, Clint had to admit, "I don't know. From where I stood, it looked like he might have wanted to kill everyone in that tent."

"Why would he want to do that?"

"I don't know," Clint said, "but I might be just the man to find out."

TWENTY-EIGHT

Clint sat in the empty wagon for a good portion of the day. Some food and water were brought to him, but they were simply slipped inside the flap by a pair of unknown hands. As the light from outside was beginning to fade, another cup and plate were brought to him. This time, however, it was brought by someone who did more than just reach into the wagon.

Fawn slipped inside and rushed to where Clint was sitting. "Why didn't you leave?" she asked.

Accepting the food before it was dropped, Clint replied, "I thought you'd be happy to see me."

"You could be killed at any moment."

"I don't think so. Besides, I could always escape again."

"Not with my help," Fawn told him. "I would have been in danger if anyone knew what I did."

"You're still just talking about untying my hands?"

She blushed a bit, but continued with even more urgency in her voice. "You know what I mean. Why wouldn't you just go?"

"I came along to the first meeting to try and stop the attacks. I think I can still help out in that regard."

"How would you plan on doing that?"

The food Fawn had brought him was a simple mixture of grains that formed a thick sort of oatmeal. Although it didn't look like much, it tasted fine and filled the void in Clint's stomach. The water he washed it down with was cool and clean.

"Where did all these people come from?" Clint asked. "Mingan says they were all from different tribes."

She nodded quickly while flinching at every sound that came from outside. "Not all from different tribes, but a few. Most of us are stragglers who got away after the rest of our people were moved to a reservation or killed."

"And the attacks? Do you know about those?"

"Ahiga says our warriors are striking back for what was done to the rest of our tribes. Even he knows that Tolfox is just out to get as much money or horses or . . . or whatever else he can. He is a thief and nothing more. That is why the Crow won't even take him back."

"He's a Crow?"

She nodded. "He was. Now he has no tribe. I suppose that makes him one of us after all." Twisting around in response to the sound of approaching footsteps, Fawn looked back at Clint with something close to panic in her eyes. "Ahiga carries your gun as a trophy, but I know your horse is still here. He is a fine animal and—"

"I know all that already. I'm not going anywhere yet."

"Why are you so stubborn?"

"Why do you want to be rid of me so badly?" Clint shot back with a smirk.

Before she could respond to that, Fawn jumped as the cover of the back of the wagon was snapped aside. Two Indians stood there, blocking out the waning light as well as any view of the rest of the camp. Both men glared at Clint and Fawn with equal amounts of disdain. Neither one was dressed in the same colors as the other men Clint had seen throughout the camp.

The larger of the two men was holding a Henry rifle

decorated with black feathers. He locked eyes with Fawn and snarled, "Get out."

Fawn lowered her head and backed out of the wagon. She looked up for a split second to see Clint before she was pushed aside by the man with the Henry.

The second Indian might not have been as large as his companion, but he wasn't a small man. His frame was slender and wiry, making him look more like a cat than a bull. "So," he said as he stepped inside, "you are the white man who tried to kill me?"

"No," Clint replied in a steady voice. "That man's dead. Just like I thought you were."

Tolfox squinted and studied Clint's face before nodding. "So you truly are the Gunsmith."

"And you truly are nothing more than a thief. At least these attacks are making a bit more sense. Last time I saw you, you were stealing cattle from herds heading through the Dakota Territories and selling them back to their owners. Is that why the Crow booted you out?"

"They'll speak my name as a hero when they hear how many Army men I've killed." Stepping forward while removing a pistol from his belt, Tolfox added, "And plenty of your own people will surely be glad to know you were killed as well."

TWENTY-NINE

The Indian with the Henry rifle grabbed Clint's arm and hauled him to his feet. Clint put up a bit of a struggle, but knew it would be pointless to do much more than that. He was going where Tolfox wanted him to go and there wasn't a lot to be done about it.

Clint was shoved outside, where Tolfox fell into step in front of him like a general touring a battlefield.

"If you want to live a bit longer, you'll take me directly to Colonel Farelli," Tolfox said.

"You already told me I was going to be killed," Clint pointed out. "Why should I help you?"

"There are easy ways to die and terrible ones. If you play your cards right, you may get an easy death or you may be set free. If things go well enough, I'll be celebrating too much to worry about spilling your blood."

"Fine," Clint said. "I'll take you there."

Tolfox stopped and stared at Clint's face. "You change your alliances that easily?"

"Do I have any other choice?"

"No," Tolfox said with a grin. "I suppose you don't."

"But I want someone else to come along with us," Clint added. "Just to make sure you don't try to pull anything."

"You truly think anyone here is on your side, white man? Who would you have join us?"

Since there were plenty of warriors standing about to watch Tolfox's little procession, Clint looked them over and settled upon one of the central figures. "Him," he said while nodding toward Ahiga.

Tolfox chuckled. "Maybe not a wise choice, but I'll accept." He waved toward Ahiga and continued walking to the spot where the horses were corralled. "Come along, Ahiga. If a fight is what you're after, you're in luck tonight."

There was no mistaking the expression on Ahiga's face. He grimaced as if he'd swallowed a chunk of rotten meat, but he broke away from his group and followed Tolfox to the horses.

"Why the new name?" Clint asked. "In the Dakotas, you were known as Proud Fox. You lose your pride somewhere along the way?"

"You palefaces are ignorant," Tolfox said. "I have always been Proud Fox, but a cavalry officer did not know our language well enough so he called me Tall Fox. An even more ignorant Army man couldn't even get that right."

"I suppose that would be Farelli?" Clint asked.

Tolfox actually smiled at that. "You would be right."

All of the Indians picked out their horses from the ones tied to the nearby posts and Clint walked straight over to Eclipse. The only thing left on the Darley Arabian's back was the saddle. Clint just hoped his saddlebags were somewhere in the camp and hadn't just been pitched somewhere between the camp and the spot of the first attack.

"What do you expect me to do on this outing?" Clint asked.

"You'll ride in front of all of us," Tolfox said. "You'll lead us to Farelli and motion for him to hold his fire."

"And if he doesn't hold his fire, I catch the first bullets?"

"That would be very helpful."

Clint pulled in a breath and climbed into his saddle. Despite everything else that had happened or was about to happen, it felt good to have Eclipse's reins back in his hands. As they rode away from the camp, Clint and Ahiga went to the front of the group while Tolfox and his tribesmen stayed a few paces behind.

"Do I at least get a weapon?" Clint asked.

Ahiga smirked. "Do you think we are stupid, white man?"

"It was worth a try. So I'm supposed to take you back to Farelli?"

"Yes."

"If I'm to lead us anywhere, I need to know where we're coming from."

"You remember where our first meeting was supposed to happen?" Ahiga asked.

"Yes."

"We're about four miles south of there."

Clint did some quick figuring and got a rough idea of where they needed to go. Fortunately, Ahiga had already pointed him in the proper basic direction.

THIRTY

Eclipse covered the flat, rocky ground as if he expected to make a run for freedom at any second. Clint could feel the anticipation in the stallion's muscles and could almost read Eclipse's anxious thoughts. But no matter how much Clint would have liked to give that order, he knew he wouldn't make it far before one or all of the Indians dropped him from his saddle.

As they rode, the sky became darker. The land stretched out in front of Clint like a gritty tapestry, broken up only by the occasional ridge or cluster of trees. There was a large, bright moon in the sky, which made the ride that much easier. Ahiga guided his own horse with a hand that was so sure, Clint wondered if the Navajo could somehow see better at night.

Clint motioned toward Ahiga the instant he picked out some movement in the distance. When he got a questioning glare from Ahiga, Clint said, "There're some riders up ahead."

"I see them," Ahiga replied.

"They're Army."

"How do you know?"

Making a quick swipe of his hand, Clint explained,

"They're riding in a search formation. They're probably looking for us."

Ahiga's voice dropped to an intent snarl. "I think they've already found us."

Already, the horses in the distance were turning from their original course to come toward Clint and Ahiga. Before Clint could say another word, the distant riders split into two groups to head in opposite directions. They were flanking the Indians.

When he looked over at Ahiga, Clint saw the big Indian already had a rifle in his hand. A gentle nudge with one leg was all it took for Clint to bring Eclipse a bit closer to the Navajo. Clint waited until Ahiga looked over at him before reaching out with one hand to grab hold of the Indian's gun.

Clint's fingers closed around the middle of Ahiga's rifle and tightened like a steel trap. Ahiga tried to pull the weapon back, but couldn't shake Clint loose. Now that he was slipping a bit in his saddle, Clint hung on to keep from falling as well as to arm himself. Fortunately, Eclipse moved as if he knew exactly what Clint had in mind and stayed beneath him as Clint struggled with Ahiga.

The big Navajo was every bit as strong as he looked. His own horse also moved to stay beneath him, making the struggle between the two men seem more like it was taking place on foot instead of thundering over a darkening landscape. Ahiga gritted his teeth and pulled to reclaim his weapon, but Clint wasn't about to let go. For a moment, it seemed Clint was faltering so Ahiga took advantage by pulling the rifle again.

Quickly correcting himself in the saddle, Clint loosened his grip when he knew Ahiga would be pulling with all his strength. That way, the Indian got little resistance and was caught off his guard. Ahiga fell back a ways and had to scramble to keep from falling off the other side of his horse. When his attention was focused on regaining his balance, Ahiga felt Clint resume the tug-of-war.

This time, Clint didn't pretend to falter and he didn't let Ahiga make a move. Clint felt the Indian wobbling a bit, so he leaned all the way back and pulled the rifle toward him. Even though he could have made the same mistake Ahiga had just made, Clint braced himself a little better and managed to take the rifle away from Ahiga. As soon as the weapon was in his possession, Clint tapped his heels against Eclipse's sides and leaned down low over the stallion's neck.

Shots were being fired and they weren't all coming from the Army riders. It seemed the Indians behind Clint had seen him make his move and were intent on stopping him. Fortunately, Clint had picked his spot well and didn't have far to go before he could position himself behind a few trees. Bullets whipped through the air past him and a few came awfully close to their mark before Clint steered Eclipse hard to the left and circled around the trees.

Clint didn't even bother taking a close look at the rifle in his hands. It was decorated with a few simple beaded straps and feathers and he could tell it was loaded. That was all he truly needed to know. By the time he circled around the other side of the trees, he knew the Indians had bigger worries than catching up to him.

Navajo and Crow alike let out yelping battle cries as beating hooves rumbled toward each other and more shots crackled through the air. Clint managed to circle around to the side of the spot where the Indians clashed with the first group of Army riders. Taking a moment to recall where the second group had split off, Clint looked around and spotted the remaining Army riders as they charged toward the Indians' flank.

Although it went against all of his instincts at that moment, Clint sat up tall in his saddle and held his rifle high over his head. Fortunately, the second group of Army riders seemed more focused on sneaking up to the battle than announcing their position. The riders headed straight toward Clint and held their fire long enough to get a look at him.

"I'm Clint Adams!" he shouted. "Don't shoot!"

The Army riders thundered up to where Clint had stopped. Most of them kept going, but a couple stayed behind to surround him. Both riders kept their guns drawn and pointed at Clint.

"Toss that rifle!" the first rider said.

Clint did as he was told while the rider closed the distance between them. The second rider got behind Clint and covered him from there. As the battle continued nearby, both of the Army riders kept their eyes and aim on Clint. Finally, Ahiga let out a distinctive yelp and the beating of hooves became louder than the gunfire.

The Indians moved away and then scattered in different directions, forcing the Army riders to split up or let some of them go. The soldiers held their ranks and stayed in one group, while the two with Clint stayed where they were.

Only after things quieted down for good did either of the men with Clint say anything.

"You were supposed to be dead," the soldier said.

Clint let out a breath and replied, "I thought you'd be glad to find me."

THIRTY-ONE

Although the soldiers didn't keep their guns aimed at him, Clint was taken back to Fort Winstead as something less than a returning comrade. At first, only Clint and his two escorts were approaching the fort. By the time they reached the front gate, however, the rest of the soldiers weren't far behind.

If Clint was expecting anyone to greet him with a hint of friendliness, he knew he would have to wait a bit longer once he saw Colonel Farelli stomp out of his shack with his hands placed firmly upon his hips.

"Where in the hell have you been, Adams?" Farelli asked.

Clint swung down from his saddle and wiped some of the sweat from his brow. "Good to see you too, Colonel."

"Cut that bullshit. Come in here and tell me what the hell happened!"

Following the colonel into the shack, Clint watched to see if he would still have an escort. The other men who'd been out riding that night were too tired to volunteer for that duty. They swapped a few words with each other, but either made their way to the saloon or dragged themselves to the bunkhouse.

As soon as Clint was inside the shack, Farelli slammed the door shut behind him. "Start explaining yourself, Adams."

"I haven't seen anyone else who was sent out with Lieutenant McGurn," Clint said.

"That's because none of them made it back."

"None of them?"

"Are you deaf? None of them!"

Clint sat down and tried to smother the anger that was flaring up inside him every time Farelli barked at him like he was punishing a child. "We got to the meeting place. The Indians were there and everything seemed to be going the way—"

"What about the chief?" Farelli cut in. "Was Chief Tolfox there, too?"

"Yes, sir. He was there. In fact, he was in the same tent with McGurn when Nolan opened fire on the whole damn place."

Farelli's eyes narrowed, but he didn't start yelling again. On the contrary, he sat down behind his desk, reached into a drawer, and pulled out a bottle half full of whiskey. "I need a drink. What about you, Adams?"

Under any other circumstance, Clint would refuse whiskey without a thought. But since this was the first time Farelli seemed to ease up around him, Clint wasn't about to turn his nose up at the offer. He accepted the whiskey and passed it under his nose. He wasn't an expert on the subject, but it smelled expensive.

"How long have you known McGurn?" Farelli asked.

Clint shrugged. "It's been a while, and we've only met a handful of times."

"Then you may or may not know he's been a pain in my ass for a long time. He's gone so far as to spread the word around here that I didn't earn my promotions. You know, on the battlefield, I could have him shot for saying such a thing."

"Maybe, but this isn't a battlefield."

"It has been ever since those Injuns declared war on me. You know how I got promoted this far up the chain?"

"I've been wondering about that."

Either Farelli didn't pick up on the sarcasm in Clint's voice or he didn't care about it, because he kept talking without a hitch. "I cleaned up not just one other area of an Indian menace, but two. Hell, I even had a lot to do with a third, but some other officer got credit for that. You know how McGurn made his rank?"

Clint shook his head.

"By riding on patrols and spending months out in the wilderness. You know what I call that?" Farelli asked. "A trapper. A scout. Not a soldier. Can you believe that?"

"And what about Nolan?" Clint asked.

Farelli shook his head and sipped his drink. "He's been at war with the Indians for years. He could probably smell an ambush coming."

"You think he'd want to kill Proud Fox?"

"Only if that bastard had something set up that would kill the lieutenant and all of his men." Motioning toward Clint with enough force to spill some of his whiskey, Farelli added, "That includes you, you know."

Clint nodded. "I know."

"So where were you these last few days? Everyone around here thought you were dead."

"I tried to tip the scales back in our favor at the meeting, but it was too late. I got knocked in the back of the head, woke up in an Indian camp with a headache to beat all, and I agreed to ride with the Indian scouts just so I could get close enough to make my move. Once I saw my chance, I broke free and met up with some of your men. I'd appreciate it if you called them in here. They're the ones that deserve a drink."

"I'm sure you'll find them in the saloon." Farelli leaned forward in his chair and asked, "Do you think you could remember where that camp is?"

"I should be able to find my way there again."

"Did you happen to pick up on anything else while you were among those savages?"

"Sure," Clint replied. "I know they're getting ready to pull up stakes and move again real soon. I also know that chief has got something he wants to deliver to the Federals and he's sure not about to hand it over to anyone around here."

"You mean Tolfox?"

Clint nodded slowly, noting how Farelli drifted right back into calling the Crow Tolfox after having slipped up not too long ago. "That's the chief I mean."

"What's he got?"

"I don't know. I wasn't exactly in a good spot to ask, but I might just be able to find out."

THIRTY-TWO

Clint headed for the only place in Fort Winstead that served liquor and hosted card games on a regular basis. Since there wasn't any competition in the immediate area, the place was marked with a sign that simply read: Saloon. And since Farelli had steered him toward the place, the colonel didn't bother watching Clint once it was clear where he was going.

Without being obvious about it, Clint made sure the colonel wasn't keeping too close an eye on him. A few more precautions made Clint fairly certain he wasn't being watched by anyone else. Therefore, he felt fairly secure when he just gave the soldiers who'd brought him in a quick wave and then walked over to a table near the back of the saloon.

"You look nervous," Abigail said as Clint sat down across from her.

He sighed and said, "You would, too, if you were walking in tall grass with so many snakes about."

"That bad, huh?"

Catching the bartender's eye, Clint pointed to the soldiers he'd waved at before and had a round of beers sent over to them. He turned his attention back to Abigail and spoke in a lower voice. "I'll know a bit more before too long. Will you be here for a while longer?"

"At least for another night. The bunkhouse isn't exactly set up for proper guests, so the colonel arranged for me to sleep in one of the rooms reserved for visiting officers. It's free and just as nice as that fancy hotel from before."

"And I doubt any officers will be visiting this place anytime soon," Clint added. "Have you been keeping busy?"

She shrugged and chewed on her lower lip.

"You look guilty," he said.

"I ain't guilty of nothin'!" she replied quickly. Realizing she'd raised her voice a bit, she brought it down a few notches and told him, "The colonel paid a hell of a lot of money for finding you and he's made it known he could have some more work real soon. I thought I'd see if I might be able to pick up some more work."

"Nothing wrong with that. You do realize this work could be messier than you're used to?"

"Yeah, I know. I ain't accepted none of it yet."

Clint couldn't help but admire the convincing half-scowl Abigail put on when she talked. The way she gripped her drink made it seem as if she wasn't sure she was going to lift the mug to her lips or smash it against someone's head. "What's the word been about this work Farelli's offering?" Clint asked. "Does it involve riding or shooting?"

"Maybe a little of both. Whatever it is, there's bound to be dustups with the Injuns. That much was made real clear."

"Well, you might just be in a position to do me a little favor."

"That's funny," she said with a grin. "I was thinking the same about you."

"What do you think about Farelli?"

The smile that had appeared on Abigail's face drifted away as quickly as it had arrived. "His money spends."

"So if you were to ask some more about these jobs he's looking to have done, would you mind letting me know what they involve?"

"And then what?" she asked suspiciously.

"And then . . . I don't know. That's it, really. I'd be mighty grateful to know what he might be planning."

"Do you think it's something bad?"

"To be honest, I can't say for certain. It might be something that has nothing to do with what I'm thinking about. For a man like Farelli to somehow find his way to the rank of colonel, he's got to have a lot of irons in the fire. Some of them have got to be official, but most of them probably aren't. He's definitely got something going on with the Indians who have been making these attacks, but the deeper I dig, the more gnarled it all becomes."

"I'll have a look-see, but I can't promise anything," she told him. "No matter what I find, you'll owe me big and I aim to collect."

"Name it."

After a bit of thought, Abigail replied, "Meet me back here in an hour or two. I should have something for ya by then."

"Great," Clint said with a nod. "Now if you'll excuse me, I need to dig a little deeper."

THIRTY-THREE

As Clint stepped outside of the fort's front gate, the only things he could hear were the crunch of his boots against the dirt and the banjo player who'd started playing inside the saloon. There were guards posted here and there, but none of them did anything besides nod when they saw Clint stroll from the fort. Even though Clint wasn't in the Army, the sorry state of Fort Winstead's patrols was disgusting.

All Clint had to do was walk over the first ridge to put himself outside of the sentry's notice. To his surprise, Clint realized that Ahiga had crept in even closer than that without being noticed. The big Navajo acknowledged Clint with a wave and worked his way back to meet him over the ridge.

"I could have snuck into that place and solved our problem right now," Ahiga muttered.

"Actually, I bet you could have snuck in there easily. This fort isn't the problem, though. It's the assholes that are keeping it up and running. Well . . . barely up and running. Did the others try to follow me?"

Ahiga shook his head. "The Crow don't speak to us unless Tolfox tells them to and I told my own braves the truth."

Smirking, Clint asked, "You know his name is Proud Fox, right?"

"Yes, but the other name rattles in his head like a . . ." After taking a moment to search for the right words, Ahiga finally said, "Like a bee in his bonnet."

Clint chuckled more at the sound of those words coming from someone like Ahiga than the actual words themselves. "I'll bet it does. And your braves know that you wanted to let me go so I could talk to the colonel?"

"They knew they were supposed to let you go. Since I was the one telling them this, they didn't ask any more than that."

"And you were able to speak with Tolfox?"

Ahiga nodded. "He stormed in when I was speaking to Mingan, strutting as he always does. When I asked to speak with him alone, Tolfox swelled up like the proud fool he is."

"And?"

Furrowing his brow was all Ahiga needed to do for Clint to know he was uncomfortable with saying any more just then. "All right," Clint said. "I'll let you know what the colonel had to say first. He's covering the tracks of the man who started the shooting, that's for certain."

"Did he order the shooting?"

No matter how many suspicions Clint had or how many suspicions were turning out to be true, Clint knew that question was most definitely loaded. "I don't know for certain yet. I do know that he's got a history with Tolfox that stretches all the way back to before that name took root. Either that, or he knows Tolfox well enough to fall into the habit of calling him Proud Fox instead. Farelli slipped up and mentioned that name without blinking an eye."

"So he could have been trying to kill his own soldiers instead of Tolfox?" Ahiga asked.

"That doesn't seem likely. Someone who gets ahead by cheating and double-dealing isn't the sort to throw murder into the mix."

"Something like that would not bother Tolfox," Ahiga stated. "All of the Crow are killers and thieves."

Now it was Clint's turn to furrow his brow. "Is that a fact or is that just some bad blood talking?"

Ahiga started to answer that without thinking, but paused and then lowered his head slightly. "Before being forced to ride away from my tribe and join this one, I was at war with the Crow. I have spent too much time with Tolfox, however, and I know he is a killer. He leads us into attacks on wagons or settlers for no good reason and then says we need to go into hiding."

"What about Mingan?" Clint asked. "That doesn't seem like his way."

"It is not. But Tolfox's men follow Tolfox and they attack without question. After that, there is no other choice but to hide."

"Hide from soldiers, you mean?"

Ahiga nodded.

"When was the first time Tolfox suggested an attack like this one?"

"A few years ago," Ahiga replied. "I was new to this mixed tribe and ready to fight any white man in a blue uniform."

"Was one of those men Farelli?"

Without hesitation, Ahiga nodded. "I stood beside Tolfox when he spoke with Farelli and struck a peace."

"I'll bet that's right about the time when Farelli started getting promoted. That could explain how Farelli got so much recognition when all he does is take up space on a chair. In fact, it's not even a new idea. I just don't think anyone's set anything up that caused this much trouble just so they could come in and look like a hero squaring it away."

Ahiga let out a breath that sounded like something close to a growl. "You and I are straw men, Adams. I have felt like one for some time and now I see you are the same."

"Straw men?"

"We are not told what we need to know, so we may be kept weak. That way, when the fight comes, we are easily knocked down by whoever comes along."

"Straw men," Clint said. "Something set up just so it can burn."

"Some among us have known that Tolfox holds secret council with the soldiers, but others don't want to believe it. And even if they do believe, there is nothing for them to do about it. Nowhere for them to go. We are a mixed tribe because we are all hunted by the soldiers or cast out by our own. There is nothing left for us."

Clint placed his hand on the Navajo's shoulder. Although the Indian warrior tensed at that, he didn't pull away. "Whatever trouble your tribe is in, it will only get worse if you just keep following Tolfox. He'll lie to you and use you all up until he gets you all killed."

"For some warriors, that is the only place for our path to lead."

"Well, it doesn't have to be that way. Are you truly telling me you and your men would die for Tolfox?"

Ahiga didn't say anything, but the dark shadow that fell over his face said more than enough.

"Of course you wouldn't," Clint said. "Just like there's no way in hell I'd die for Farelli."

"But it seems that he wanted it to be that way."

"Yeah," Clint said as that truth settled in like a stone at the bottom of his stomach. "But just because we've been used as straw men doesn't mean we have to give up and burn. Farelli is already resigned to sitting with his feet up in this pile of firewood he calls a fort and knows that he's finished if any real officers find out what he's doing. All we need to do is get some proof."

"When you told me you wanted to get away and meet with Farelli, you said you would lead him back to us."

"And I did," Clint said. "I told him I'd take him to your camp. Is everyone ready to move?"

"We have already moved. All that is left are the crippled wagons." With a foul look on his face, Ahiga added, "Sleeping there was like sleeping in a white man's trash heap."

"Well, there probably won't be much left. Did you make the arrangements we agreed upon?"

Ahiga grinned. "And one of my scouts has found someone who could be an ace in the hole."

After hearing who Ahiga had found, Clint was the one grinning. "Good," he said. "Now we can see who the straw men really are."

THIRTY-FOUR

After arranging another meeting along with some individual tasks, Clint strolled back toward the fort and Ahiga slipped away to blend in with the shadows. The Navajo moved like a large cat, keeping his head down and his arms stretched in front of him to avoid being surprised by a rock or bush.

Catching the eye of a guard near the front gate, Clint tossed the soldier a wave and kept walking. He had a lie on the tip of his tongue and ready to fly, but didn't even need it. The soldier returned Clint's wave with a nod and went back to whatever dream had been occupying his attention. Clint had heard soldiers talk about having the military in their blood, but hadn't thought much about that for himself. Perhaps he did have some military blood, because Clint still wanted to whip those lazy soldiers into shape even though he didn't have an official rank of his own.

The saloon was almost as busy as a proper gambling hall in a good-sized town. It seemed more soldiers were in there than at their posts or doing any real work. Then again, with a commanding officer like Farelli, it was a wonder that any work in Fort Winstead got done at all.

Clint was looking around at the various faces inside the saloon when he felt a tug on his sleeve.

"You Clint Adams?" the bartender asked as he leaned back behind the bar.

Straightening the sleeve the barkeep had pulled, Clint replied, "I am."

"One of the officers wants to have a word with ya."

"Farelli?"

"Nah," the bartender replied with a shake of his head. "Some other one."

"Who?"

The bartender shrugged his shoulders angrily and turned to get back to his conversation with a drunken private. This time, he was the one who was interrupted by a tug on his sleeve. When he turned around, he saw Clint staring back at him.

"Where's this officer at?" Clint asked.

"Outside and to the right."

Rather than impose upon the bartender any further, Clint stepped outside and turned right. There wasn't much to see there, other than a few hitching posts and a small house that was maintained enough to look distinctly out of place within the walls of Fort Winstead. But what jumped out at him more than the house was the horse tied to the post outside that house. It was a white mustang with brown spots.

Clint knocked on the door, which was enough to push it open an inch or two.

"Come on in," a bespectacled clerk in a tidy blue uniform replied. He held the door open and then pushed it shut once Clint was inside.

"Is this where the visiting officers are allowed to stay?" Clint asked.

"Yes. Are you one of Colonel Farelli's guests?"

Unable to help himself, Clint replied, "Why, yes. Do I get a room for the night?"

"Just go right up those stairs. Only one other room's occupied, so you can take your pick from the rest. There's blankets and sheets available, so let me know if you need anything else."

Clint might have heard those words, but he was already at the top of the stairs when the clerk finished his sentence. The slender young man with the spectacles must have been used to being treated that way, so he merely shouted the remainder of his instructions up the stairs and then went back to whatever he'd been doing before. In fact, Clint thought his rude manner might have helped put him over as an officer. At least the clerk didn't seem at all interested in following him up the stairs.

Just like any other house its size, this one had a narrow hallway at the top of the stairs, which led to several narrow doorways. All but one of those doors were halfway open, so Clint went straight to the one that was closed and tried the handle. After opening that door just enough to make his presence known, Clint leaned toward it and whispered, "It's Clint. Don't shoot."

"Well, come in, then," Abigail replied.

Clint stepped inside and found himself in a small yet tidy bedroom. Most of the space was taken up by the bed, itself, and Abigail was taking up a good amount of the space beneath the blankets. She lay on her side, using one hand to prop up her head. With her other hand, she pulled the blankets off to reveal that she wasn't wearing a stitch of clothes.

"You owe me big, Adams," she said. "Time for me to collect."

THIRTY-FIVE

"Looks like you've already washed up," Clint said as he unbuttoned his shirt and let his eyes wander along the smooth contours of Abigail's body.

"Just get those clothes off and come here," she demanded.

Clint smiled and hurried to undress, but stopped just short of removing his jeans. "You said I owe you. What did you find out?"

"The colonel's planning on riding out to hang a whole bunch of Injuns."

"He's going, himself?"

Still holding the blanket up, she nodded. Abigail's hair fell in a loose tousle over her face and her legs shifted beneath her body. Just keeping that blanket and her head propped up was enough to put the taut lines of her muscles on display. "He's leading some sort of charge and he's mighty proud of it. I know he's telling the truth because he's hiring on anyone he can to ride ahead and clear a path for him."

"Is he more interested in guns or scouts?"

"He's not interested in doing anything until an hour before sunrise, so get over here before I kick you out of my damn room."

The moment Clint got close enough for her to reach him, Abigail grabbed him by the waistband of his jeans and pulled him to the bed. Clint slapped her hand away so he could get undressed the rest of the way, which seemed to stoke the fire that was already burning within Abigail. By the time Clint was out of his clothes, she was on her knees and at the edge of the mattress.

Abigail wrapped one arm around the back of Clint's neck so she could pull him close and kiss him fiercely on the lips. Her other hand slid down between his legs, where she began stroking his cock until it was good and hard.

Pulling his head back just enough to break the kiss, Clint returned the favor by grabbing a handful of hair at the back of her head so he could hold her still as he kissed her again. Abigail loved his rough manner every bit as much as he thought she would. Her lips parted and she slipped her tongue into Clint's mouth. She pressed her naked body against him and trembled as soon as his rigid penis brushed against the lips of her pussy.

She was dripping wet between her legs. With her hand still on him, she guided Clint to her warm opening and let out a moan the instant he began to slip into her. With Abigail on her knees upon the edge of the bed and Clint standing on the floor next to the bed, he couldn't enter her more than an inch or so. Abigail spread her legs apart as much as she could, while reaching around to grab Clint's hip and pull him closer.

Clint placed his hands upon her backside and ran the other hand up along her breasts. She had a strong, muscular body, and responded with a louder groan when Clint's fingers found her nipples. Clint rolled the sensitive flesh of her nipple between thumb and forefinger, ending with a little pinch to make Abigail pull in a quick, excited breath.

"Oh, Lord, you make me crazy." She sighed as she backed away so she could lie down upon the bed and open her legs for him.

Clint didn't waste any time in climbing onto the bed, but Abigail was too anxious to wait for even a second. Her hands were drifting over her own body. With one hand she played with the nipple Clint had been teasing and she rubbed the other hand over her glistening clitoris.

As soon as Clint lowered himself on top of her, he felt Abigail's legs wrap around him and lock in tight. She wrapped her arms around him as well, shifting her hips until she felt his cock slide to where it needed to be.

"That's it." She sighed as Clint pushed all the way into her. "Just like that."

Once Clint started pumping in and out of her, he could feel Abigail squirming in time to his rhythm. Her strong hips thrust back and forth, urging him to slam harder and harder into her. Soon, Clint grabbed hold of one of Abigail's hands and tightened his grip as he needed to hold on to something to keep from being tossed out of the bed. His other hand slid down and around to cup her firm backside as he continued to drive into her like a piston.

Suddenly, Abigail pressed her face against Clint's shoulder and hung on with both arms wrapped around him. She writhed and pumped herself along his cock until a powerful orgasm shook her from head to toe. When it subsided, she leaned back and stretched both arms out to spread her hair out behind her head. Looking up at Clint, she said, "I've been waiting for that since the last time."

"Well," Clint said as he straightened up so he was kneeling between her legs, "it's not over yet."

Her eyes widened expectantly and an excited smile appeared on her face as Clint cupped her backside in both hands so he could position her just right and lift her a little ways up off the bed. As soon as she felt Clint's hard column of flesh once more against the soft lips of her pussy, Abigail propped herself up for him and waited to feel him impale her.

Clint's erection parted her smooth skin and slipped

back into the warmth of her body. Still kneeling so his back was straight and she was lying flat upon the bed, Clint grabbed on to her hips and held her up as he slowly moved in and out of her. Abigail stretched languidly along the bed as Clint's thrusts became more and more powerful. Soon, he was rocking her with enough force to inch her toward the other edge of the mattress.

Arching his back as he settled into a good rhythm, Clint knew he'd hit a good spot when he felt Abigail's entire body start to shake. He watched her face as she turned her head to one side and bucked her hips while grabbing on to the blankets. When her orgasm came, it made her pull in a breath and become perfectly quiet for a few seconds. In that time, Clint felt her pussy tighten around his cock in a way that pushed him even closer to his own edge.

She went over that edge first, but Clint was right behind her.

THIRTY-SIX

Clint was able to get a little rest before he had to leave Abigail's room. When he crept down the stairs, hoping not to see anyone along the way, he felt like a boy sneaking away from home to go into town. Since the clerk in the officer's guest quarters didn't seem to know what was going on beyond his own desk, Clint didn't take too many extra precautions. As it was, Clint was able to get outside and to Eclipse without drawing much attention.

Abigail had been right in her assessment that any soldier worth his salt had been recruited for Colonel Farelli's special assignment. That meant only the lazy, drunk, and worthless soldiers were left behind to guard the fort. And that, in turn, meant Clint could come and go however he pleased.

Once he'd walked Eclipse through the front gates, Clint snapped the reins and built up speed until the Darley Arabian was at a full gallop. The sky was still dark, but he could taste the approaching dawn in the back of his throat. There was a crispness in the air and a subtle glow at the edge of the eastern horizon. It would be dawn soon, so Clint knew Farelli and his men would be out in force before too much longer.

The last time he'd met with Ahiga, Clint made an arrangement with the big Navajo that involved a certain number of Indians staying behind while the rest of the tribe moved on to a safer place. That small group of warriors wasn't far from the fort, but they'd picked a spot that was supposed to grant them the advantage over any of the soldiers. Clint figured Ahiga knew what he was doing, but even he didn't expect to be taken by surprise as easily as this.

Before he had a chance to hear the sound of approaching horses or see a hint of movement, Clint was surrounded on three sides by Indians. The man directly in front of him was Ahiga, himself.

"Where are the rest of you?" Clint asked as he struggled to rein Eclipse to a stop.

Remaining perfectly still even though the Darley Arabian stallion was charging straight toward him, Ahiga watched with mild interest until Eclipse slowed to a halt. "The rest of the tribe is safe," Ahiga said.

"What about these two?" Clint asked as he shot a quick glance to each of the other Indians.

"They can be trusted."

"Where's Tolfox?"

"He thinks he is guarding the rest of the tribe by watching us from afar. I know exactly where he is and where he will be looking, so I know he won't be able to see us now."

Clint had his doubts about that one, but he let them go since it didn't really matter if Tolfox knew he was there or not. "You think he'll do anything once the rest of the tribe has their backs to him?" he asked.

Ahiga shook his head. "Since his own people are among the tribe, I think he will do his best to protect them."

"Has he ever done anything to make you think he might hurt your people?" Clint asked.

Ahiga considered that for a moment and replied, "He cannot be trusted, but I have told some of those that are close to Mingan about what we are doing here. If Tolfox or any of those other Crow step out of line, they will be stricken down."

"All right, then. When I left the fort, Farelli and his men were still there," Clint reported. "We should have just enough time to make our preparations. We just need to make sure everyone's in the right place at the right time. How's our ace in the hole doing?"

Clint had only seen Ahiga smile a couple times and it was never a pretty sight. This time was no exception. "He is feeling better. It shouldn't take long to bring him all the way around to our way of thinking."

"Well, just keep him safe and make sure he's where he needs to be when the time comes."

It only took another minute or so for Clint and Ahiga to outline what they had in mind to the other two Navajo. Once that was done, Clint pointed Eclipse back toward the fort and raced away. The Navajo went in the other direction and disappeared almost as quickly as they'd appeared.

Clint tapped his heels against Eclipse's sides and gave the reins a snap every couple of seconds. The Darley Arabian responded perfectly and didn't let up on his pace until they were almost through the front gates of Fort Winstead. As Clint drew closer, he could see a large group of horsemen emerging from the fort. Colonel Farelli led that group as if he were at the head of a parade.

"Adams!" Farelli hollered.

Clint steered toward the group as Eclipse caught his breath. "Just out for a morning ride. What's the occasion?"

"We're out for a ride, ourselves. I know you already told me about that Indian camp, but it would do us a lot more good if you could take us there yourself."

"I hear there's a salary being offered to any civilians that accept this ride of yours."

Farelli nodded and grinned like he was still the belle of the ball. "Of course. And seeing as how you made this possible, I'll tack on an extra fee if you come along for the whole ride."

"I suppose I could see my way clear considering there's an extra fee involved."

"Good," Farelli said. Turning his eyes to the trail leading away from the fort, he drew his saber and pointed down the road. "Onward!"

A few soldiers moved with genuine steam in their step, but most of the others simply rode behind the colonel as if they were still rubbing the sleep from their eyes. Clint waited for a good portion of the group to file past him before finding the rider he was after and falling into step alongside the other horse.

"Trying to get a piece of the colonel's money, huh?" Abigail asked from the back of her white mustang.

Clint shrugged and shook his head. "Someone who's after nothing but money only understands greed. At least this way I'm accepted as just another hired gun."

"I don't know about that, but the colonel sure seems wrapped up in his own bullshit. Look at him up there like the cock of the walk. I give him another minute or so before he calls for us to ride ahead and make sure he doesn't get his pretty boots dirty on anything."

"His boots will be the least of his worries before too long," Clint said in a voice that was kept low enough to go unheard by anyone but Abigail.

"What have you got planned?" she asked.

"Me?" Clint replied with mock offense. "I'm just going along for the whole ride and will probably get paid enough to buy half a bottle of whiskey when it's all said and done. You, on the other hand, are going to make certain these soldiers waste all their time here before being led back toward the fort on a wild-goose chase. That sound like something you could do?"

"Half a bottle, huh? The colonel must have given you

one hell of a bonus. I'd say I got paid enough to chase a few wild geese."

Just then, Farelli's voice thundered through the air. "Scouts! Ride ahead and see how many Indians you can find. There's a bonus for any redskins you kill before I get there."

"That took longer than I thought," Abigail said as she snapped her reins and rode ahead along with the men who'd been hired on to ride with the soldiers.

Clint rode along as well. As soon as he was spotted, the rest of the scouts fell in behind him.

THIRTY-SEVEN

It wasn't long before shots crackled through the air. There were enough horses charging to or from the camp of crippled wagons to send a constant rumble through the ground. Indian braves yelped their battle cries as scouts shouted back and forth to one another.

After watching Ahiga lead his men around the camp in one direction, Clint pointed in another and shouted, "They went that way!"

The scouts had their guns drawn and had been firing, but they didn't seem too anxious to give chase now that a few bullets and arrows had sailed over their heads. Just to be certain, Clint steered Eclipse to a spot that prevented anyone from truly going after Ahiga. The scouts weren't about to trample him, so they went where Clint wanted them to go.

Colonel Farelli rode up to the camp with his pistol drawn. "Just as Adams described it," he said upon setting his sights on the grounded wagons and single tepee. "Open fire!" Without waiting for any of his men to make a move, Farelli aimed at the tepee and pulled his trigger.

Between the order from Farelli and the shots that were already being fired, the soldiers with the colonel reflexively followed their leader's example. Shots were fired one after the other until the tepee was a tattered mess and the wagons had more holes than a fishing net.

"Take no chances!" Farelli barked to the man beside him. "I want those wagons blown to bits! Where's my dynamite?"

Now that the scouts were away from the camp and riding off in the proper direction, Clint pulled on his reins and steered Eclipse toward the camp. Once the first volley of Farelli's gunfire was over, Clint heard a loud explosion and saw one of the wagons shatter into a burst of splintered wood.

Clint kept his head low and raced around the camp until he caught sight of where Ahiga was waiting for him. The Navajo was off his horse and motioned for Clint to follow suit. As soon as he was close enough, Clint swung down from the saddle and led Eclipse behind the cover of a bunch of rocks.

"Where's our ace in the hole?" Clint asked.

Ahiga reached for his own saddle to grab a large bundle that had been slung across his horse's rump. Handling the bundle as if it wasn't any heavier than a load of hay, Ahiga dropped it to the ground and pulled back the blanket to reveal the petrified face of the skinny translator. Clint looked at the translator's face and was instantly reminded of the attack that had ended Lieutenant McGurn's life.

Upon seeing the translator's face, Clint grinned and looked over to Ahiga. "I thought you were kidding when you said you'd found him."

"Why would I kid about that?"

Not wanting to take the time to explain sarcasm to the Indian, Clint shifted his focus to the translator. Fortunately, Farelli had another one of the wagons blown up right about then. "You hear that?" Clint asked.

The translator nodded vehemently and tried to cover his eyes. His arms were tied behind his back, however, so the best he could manage was to clench his eyes shut and turn his head away.

"Your Colonel Farelli has come back for you," Clint said. "Seems he truly doesn't like loose ends."

"Wh . . . what do you . . . do you want from me?" the translator stammered.

Clint grabbed the translator's chin and forced the little man to look directly at him. "Farelli doesn't know his ass from a hole in the ground, so he sure as hell doesn't know how to speak anything besides English. That means you went along for all of the talks with the Indians." When he didn't get an answer, Clint barked, "Didn't you?"

The translator nodded and then nearly jumped off the ground when another stick of dynamite was tossed.

"How long have you worked with Farelli?" Clint asked.

"I've . . . I've been with the colonel since . . . I've . . ." Whenever the translator started to speak, he was cut short by more gunfire and the pounding of hooves as a group of Indians caught the soldiers' attention.

Clint looked up to Ahiga and saw the Navajo toss him a short wave. "My braves are drawing fire," Ahiga said. "Nothing more."

"Keep talking," Clint said to the translator.

"I've been with the colonel for two years!"

"Go on."

Now that his tongue had been loosened, the words flowed out of him like water spilling from a bucket. "It's been two years and I wasn't allowed to transfer! The colonel said he liked working with me and he would pay me to stay on. He's paid me enough to buy a ranch for my uncle, but he still wouldn't let me go."

"I don't want to hear about your uncle," Clint snapped, "and I don't want to hear about a ranch. Tell me what you know about Farelli and Chief Tolfox."

"They've been making these arrangements for about a

year and a half. Every time they have to start over again, Tolfox takes on a new name."

"These attacks were arranged?" Clint asked.

"Yes, all of them," the translator sputtered. Suddenly, his eyes widened and he added, "Not all of them. The first one was real. Chief Proud Fox led an attack on a settlement in the Dakotas. Farelli was sent to deal with him and he offered to pay the Indians off rather than fight them. When he couldn't come up with the money, Farelli stole from the Army."

"What did he steal?" Clint asked.

"I don't know. I was only there to translate, but I saw Army wagons carrying supplies, guns, you name it. All Farelli asked was that he get the credit for it and when he got promoted, he found Proud Fox again. They would meet to arrange where the attacks would take place and when they would stop."

"What happened this time?" Clint asked.

"I don't know!" As the translator spoke, tears began streaming down his narrow face. "I swear I don't know! Please!"

Clint couldn't take it anymore. He grabbed the translator by the arms and lifted him up. "It's all right."

"No! He always sent Nolan to do his killing when he didn't want to use soldiers! I thought he might just kill Tolfox, but Farelli wanted all of us dead. Now he's blowing this whole place up just to get to me. Oh Lord, there's nowhere for us to go!"

When Clint had arranged for Ahiga to bring the translator to this spot at this time, his intention was to put the fear of God into the little fellow. Now that his plan had worked even better than he'd expected, Clint couldn't help but feel a little guilty. Keeping his scowl firmly in place, Clint looked into the translator's eyes and asked, "You want to live through this?"

"Yes, yes, oh God, please—"

"Fine," Clint interrupted. "You'll tell us everything you know about Farelli and you'll repeat all of that to whatever Army tribunal presides over his court-martial."

"All right, all right! He's trying to kill me anyway. I'll do anything!"

Looking to Ahiga, Clint said, "Take him somewhere safe. Which way would I go to catch up with Tolfox?"

"Elsu will take you."

Upon hearing his name, one of the nearby Navajo pointed his horse away from camp and waved for Clint to follow.

"You shouldn't waste time," Ahiga warned. "Elsu moves very swiftly."

THIRTY-EIGHT

Ahiga surely hadn't exaggerated his partner's love for speed. It was all Clint could do to climb into his saddle and race after the other Navajo as Ahiga dragged the translator away. In the camp, Farelli and his men seemed to be amusing themselves by laying waste to everything they could find and didn't stop until they'd blown apart each and every wagon in the area.

A few shots were fired in Clint's direction by some overly eager soldiers, but Elsu had a big head start and Eclipse wasn't rattled by any amount of gunfire. With a few quick turns and a flick of the reins, Clint had put the camp behind him and was soon well out of the soldiers' firing range.

Elsu was a slender Indian who looked to be somewhere in his late teens. His thick black hair was just past shoulder-length and the clothes he wore complemented his ability to ride like a flicker of lightning. Tanned leather britches hugged him like a second skin and the feathers tied to his arms and head fluttered in the wind as if they were still attached to a bird's wing. When he looked over his shoulder, the young Navajo smiled to find Clint so close behind him. Elsu pointed ahead and to the left.

Nodding at the younger man's signal, Clint snapped his reins and nearly closed the distance between himself and Elsu in a matter of seconds. They needed to ride for several miles, but the two horses covered the distance in a flash. Toward the end of the ride, Clint felt as if he was in a simple race instead of the web that kept getting more twisted by the moment. At least this time, Clint was the one doing the twisting.

As soon as they got within sight of the cluster of horses carrying Mingan and the rest of his tribe, Clint motioned for Elsu to slow down. Reluctantly, the young Navajo complied.

"What do you know about Tolfox?" Clint asked.

Elsu scowled and replied, "That he thinks he is the leader of our people and the only place he wants to lead us is into war."

"Do you know about his arrangement with the colonel?"

"Everyone knows about it, but nobody dares to speak against it. Tolfox leads just enough Crow to stand beside him. His braves will kill women and children. We have seen it. We do not stand against them to protect our own women and children."

"Why don't you just leave?" Clint asked.

"The same reason you go through all this trouble to ruin the colonel's attack when you could have simply ridden in the other direction."

"Fair enough, I suppose," Clint admitted. "What's the best way I can get Tolfox and his men away from the rest of the tribe?"

"Say the colonel wants to have a talk," Elsu suggested with confidence. "Tolfox will step forward with all of his men and will not allow anyone else to come."

"Is that how it's always been?"

Elsu nodded once. "Chief Mingan thought Tolfox was speaking to the colonel for the good of the tribe. This is before he knew . . ."

Knowing that the young Navajo didn't want to say anything to cast his elder in a bad light, Clint finished Elsu's thought with, "Before he knew there was a trickster in your midst?"

"That's right. Once he knew, it was too late."

"It might not be too late. Tell me one thing, and I want you to be honest with me."

"All right."

"How many have your people killed?" Clint asked. "I'm not talking about your tribe. I mean your people."

"Ahiga is He Who Fights," Elsu replied. "Ahiga has always fought, but he is no murderer. He rode with Tolfox only once. After that, he was only brought along to talk with the colonel so the white men would know we had many braves in our tribe."

"And the attacks on the wagons?"

"They were made by Tolfox and his Crow. The Crow are killers. They are the murderers."

Clint narrowed his eyes and asked, "How many Crow have you known?"

Reluctantly, Elsu lowered his head. "I have only known Tolfox and his men."

"That's right. Don't think too far ahead of yourself, boy. You deal with every man as he comes along. Let him show who he is and go from there. You understand?"

Elsu nodded.

"Good. I've already dealt with Ahiga and your Chief Mingan enough to know they're good men. I've heard and seen more than enough to know what kind of man Farelli is. Let's have a closer look at Tolfox."

THIRTY-NINE

Separating Tolfox and his men was just as easy as Elsu had predicted it would be. In fact, Clint was surprised at how easy it was. All he needed to do was catch up to the rest of the tribe and say the magic words. Once Clint announced that Farelli wanted to have a word with someone from the tribe, Tolfox stepped forward and practically shoved Mingan aside. Since Ahiga was elsewhere keeping the translator safe, only a few Navajo braves remained and they didn't want to leave the tribe unprotected.

"It's all right," Clint said to Mingan. "You should stay here with your people. Can you see them to safety?"

"Yes," the old man replied. "But—"

"There's nothing else to say," Clint cut in. "Your people need to be away from here and they need to go right now."

Mingan rode on the back of an old horse that looked strong enough to pull every last one of those wagons from the former camp. After stopping close enough for his horse and Eclipse to bump noses, Mingan whispered, "If there is talking to be done, it is time that I started doing it."

"There'll be time for that later," Clint assured him.

With Tolfox and the small group of Crow warriors nearby, Clint focused his eyes on Mingan and held that gaze for a few more seconds. It seemed that enough was said in that gaze to get Clint's point across. Mingan nodded solemnly and rode back to his people.

"Time's wasting," Tolfox said.

Clint rode past the Crow and motioned for them to follow. "Absolutely right. Let's not waste any more."

Eclipse led the way and the Crow followed. Choosing a path that separated them from both the burning camp and the straggling Navajo, Clint led Tolfox for the better part of a mile until he could feel the men behind him getting restless. Before Tolfox could ask any questions, Clint pulled back on his reins and climbed down from his saddle.

"This is the place," Clint said.

Tolfox looked around. The spot Clint had chosen was closed off by trees on one side and rocks on another. To the north, there was open land that stretched out for miles without much of anything to show for it. Every so often, the distant crackle of gunshots could be heard coming from the southeast.

"Where is the colonel?" Tolfox demanded.

"He'll be along. I figured you might want to get here before he had a chance to get his men situated."

Tolfox nodded and eventually climbed down from his own saddle. Since Clint had settled in to lean against a tree with his arms folded across his chest, it seemed they weren't going to be led anywhere else. The Crow warriors followed Tolfox's lead and dismounted as well.

After a few quiet seconds had passed, Clint said, "You know Farelli meant to kill you, right?"

"Why would he do that? Ahiga told us you were allowed to leave so you could learn what the soldiers were planning. Did you hear something about Farelli trying to kill me?"

"Oh, I heard plenty of things. I knew he would try to burn down this camp the moment he found out where it was. That is, he'd burn it down if he was trying to make sure something got buried along the way."

Furrowing his brow, Tolfox said, "If you were one of Farelli's spies, you wouldn't have sent word that the soldiers would come and we would have all been killed in that attack."

"Go on."

"If you were protecting your own skin, you would have gone away and not come back."

"Very true," Clint said.

"So that means Ahiga and Mingan were right about you. They said you wanted to help our tribe and that's all that remains."

"I do want to help the tribe. Too bad the same can't be said about you."

Upon hearing that, all four of Tolfox's men bristled. A few were armed with pistols and a couple had rifles as well. They all carried knives and every single one of them started to reach for one of their weapons.

FORTY

Tolfox extended one hand toward his men without taking his eyes away from Clint. Speaking one word in his own language, Tolfox calmed his men as if he could feel what every single one of them was about to do.

"You've been dealing with Farelli for a while now," Clint said. "What's the deal been? Were you arranging the attacks and calling them off as Farelli saw fit? How much were you getting paid?"

"I was working to help my tribe."

"You were attacking innocent families and travelers. Don't put on an act with me because I've seen what you've done. I've heard it from Farelli, himself! You and your men killed Army soldiers. How was that supposed to help your tribe?"

"We only killed soldiers when Farelli refused to pay!" Tolfox roared. "Did Farelli tell you that as well?"

Clint had to use every bit of bluffing skill he'd learned throughout the years just to keep from smiling. In order to prod the Crow leader a bit more, Clint said, "He told me you were getting greedy and that it was too dangerous to have a bloodthirsty killer on his payroll."

Tolfox gnashed his teeth so hard that Clint expected to see sparks in his mouth. "That son of a bitch wanted to pay me in old blankets and boots. He wanted me to kill for blankets and boots!"

"You did kill."

"I killed *his* men! When he tried to play me for a fool, I killed anyone wearing the uniform of his Army. And when he tried to hide from me, I killed until he had no choice but to show his cowardly face! He's shown what kind of man he is! Everyone will see!"

"I already see," Clint replied. "Just like I've seen what kind of man you are. You're the kind of man who kills women and children just to draw one fool from hiding. You kill soldiers who are trying to protect innocent folks just so you can get your hands on one crooked colonel. Throughout this whole thing, you've shown yourself to be the kind of man who doesn't even care if you send your own people to hell while you make your deals and go on your rampages."

Tolfox slapped his hand around the gun that was kept in an old holster at his side. The holster hung from braided rope looping around his waist and held a Colt that looked as if it had once belonged to a soldier. That Colt made it halfway from Tolfox's holster before Clint drew and fired a shot from his own pistol.

The modified Colt bucked once against Clint's palm and sent a round through Tolfox's ribs. It wasn't a killing shot, but it was enough to spin Tolfox around on one foot and put him into a world of pain.

The other Crow braves took aim with their own guns as well. One of them already had a rifle in hand, so Clint targeted him first. One round through the face sent that Indian flying backward off his feet as his rifle toppled through the air.

Two more Crow were bringing their gun hands up and were knocked down like bottles from a fence as Clint sent a round into each of their hearts. Before those two had the dirt, Clint had shifted his aim to the remaining Crow brave.

That Indian was obviously less experienced with firearms because he pulled his knife from the scabbard at his side instead of the pistol that was tucked into his waistband.

Clint took careful aim and gave the last Crow a warning glare before saying, "Run."

The Indian not only backed away, but he tossed aside every one of his weapons as he bolted away from the spot where the others had fallen.

Watching the fleeing Crow until he knew the Indian wasn't about to circle back and put up a fight, Clint stepped over to the man who'd caught the first bullet. Tolfox had a nasty wound in his side that looked as if a bear had swiped across his ribs with one massive claw. Seeing that Tolfox was trying to lift his gun, Clint kicked the gun away with one well-placed boot. After that, he stood just out of the Indian's reach and watched him carefully.

"This was . . . the colonel's idea," Tolfox said.

"But you and your men did the killing."

Tolfox was too tired and in too much pain to even try to lie convincingly. Instead, he clawed at the ground and said, "It was on his orders. I didn't have . . . a choice."

"Bullshit." Clint spat. "You could have made your way like anyone else. You could have done your best like any other tribe. If there was no other way to make a living, how come Chief Mingan seems perfectly capable of making a home for his people."

"I'm chief!" Tolfox snapped.

"Sure. You're a fine chief. Chief Proud Fox. Or was it Tall Fox? I forgot that it was such common practice for a worthy chief to go under so many different names. There are men who do what you do, Tolfox. There are men who kill and lie and scurry from place to place under all sorts of different names so they won't be recognized. They're called outlaws, and white men have them just like the Indians have them. That's all you are, Tolfox. You're just a murdering outlaw who takes orders from another outlaw."

"That's right," Tolfox said desperately. "I took orders. Go speak to Colonel Farelli. He's the one you should be after, not me!"

"Your English is pretty good, Tolfox. I bet that came in real handy when you were dealing with Farelli. Here, Farelli thought he needed a translator and yet you could carry on just fine in his language. Is that how you knew he was going to cheat you?"

Letting out a breath, Tolfox closed his eyes and relaxed his muscles.

"I know it took the both of you to do all this," Clint said. "You had to pull off the attacks and Farelli had to pretend to stop them. I've stopped you. I want to stop Farelli as well. Instead of lying there and hoping to bleed out, you could take some part in redeeming yourself."

"What good could I do?" Tolfox asked. "My braves are gone and your Army wouldn't listen to a word I had to say. They would hang me or shoot me like they would hang or shoot any Crow who spilled a white man's blood."

Clint hunkered down so he could talk to the fallen Indian without lording over him. "I told Farelli you had something and were taking it to the Federals. It was just a bluff to see if he'd get riled up enough to show what he was capable of, but he bit on the bait pretty damn hard. He got more than riled up. He came to that old camp you just left behind, intending to blow the place to hell no matter who was inside it. That tells me two things. First of all, it tells me that Farelli is willing to kill women and children just like you've already done. Second, it tells me there must be something you've got that can do a whole lot of damage to Farelli."

It took Tolfox a few seconds, but finally he began to nod. After that, it took him a few more second to pull enough air into his lungs to speak. "The colonel was careful not to leave a trail when he dealt with me. All of our agreements . . . were spoken. But to get Ahiga and his braves to help on some of the attacks . . . Farelli needed . . . something else."

"Something that could link him to this whole mess?" Clint asked.

"Yes. But if I tell you this . . . I need you . . . to swear . . . you won't leave me here to bleed to death like a wounded dog."

Clint wouldn't have let any man die that slowly, but there was no need to tell Tolfox that much. Instead, Clint extended a hand and helped the wounded Crow to his feet.

FORTY-ONE

Mingan couldn't hide his surprise when he saw both Clint and Tolfox ride back to the rest of the tribe. The Indians all rode with their horses clustered in a group so the braves could keep watch from the outside while protecting the children and women in the middle of the cluster. Even though Mingan rode toward the front of the group, the uneasy faces on the nearby braves made it known that they wished he would accept a bit more protection.

"Where are the others?" Mingan asked.

Tolfox slouched forward upon his horse with his head hung low. Now that he was closer, it was easier for the others to see that Tolfox's hands were tied at the wrists and his wrists were tied to the saddle horn. Blood was already soaking through the shredded material wrapped around Tolfox's ribs as a makeshift bandage.

Riding beside Tolfox so he could keep hold of the Crow's reins, Clint brought Eclipse and Tolfox's horse to a stop. "The other Crow are gone," he said. "Three were shot dead and a fourth ran away. I had to kill those three because they meant to kill me. If anyone has something to say about this, say it now."

There were plenty of uneasy glances tossed among the

Navajo, but none of them spoke out against what they'd heard.

"Tolfox is coming along with us as a prisoner," Clint announced. "He's been leading you people down a path that will only end in more blood. Farelli's on a rampage of his own at the moment, but the rest of the Army will only pick up where he leaves off if this doesn't stop right now. Agreed?"

The tribe was silent.

One by one, the Navajo all turned their eyes to one man.

Mingan accepted their silent gazes by tightening the muscles in his jaw and bowing his head a bit as if their attention weighed on him like a load of bricks. Then the old man straightened up and sat in his saddle as if he towered above all the others. "We did not have the courage to stand up to Tolfox before. We should have been the ones to stand against him now. We will take him and see to it that no more blood is spilled because of our own mistake."

Just then, Clint spotted a face among the braves that he hadn't been expecting. "Ahiga? Is that you?"

The Navajo warrior nodded once.

"So where's . . . ?" Before he could finish his question, Clint spotted the translator among the Indian women toward the center of the tribe's protective group. The skinny fellow was covered by a blanket that made him look more like an old woman. If not for the translator's distinctive face and pasty white skin, Clint might not have seen him there at all.

"I led the soldiers away," Ahiga said. "They did not follow me for long once they were done with our camp. I thought this man would be safest here with us. If you want me to take him somewhere else—"

"Oh, no," Clint interrupted. "This is fine. To be honest, I doubt he'd be much safer anywhere else." As he rode closer to Ahiga, Clint needed to fight to keep from laughing at the nervous translator who had more fear in his eyes than the women surrounding him.

Clint looked back to make certain the men who'd taken the reins to Tolfox's horse weren't having any trouble with their prisoner. Even though Tolfox's wound looked a whole lot worse than it truly was, the Crow slouched in his saddle as if all the life had been drained from him. For the moment, Tolfox wasn't going to give anyone much of a fight.

"Tolfox has done a lot of talking," Clint said to Ahiga. "Without his men, he doesn't have a lot left in him."

"Good," Ahiga replied.

"I know you're not Crow and I know most of the men in the attack I saw were painted with the same marks as Tolfox's warriors, but you were also one of the men who attacked that wagon and those soldiers a while ago."

"Yes."

"Why fight in Tolfox's battles?" Clint asked. "Especially when you already knew Tolfox was dealing with Farelli?"

Ahiga sat tall as a mountain and wore an expression that was just as stony. "Because if the colonel thought I was with him, he would not slaughter this tribe the way his Army has slaughtered so many others."

"How do you know that?"

"He wrote a letter to me, swearing this. He handed it to me personally and swore it was his bond."

"Where is that letter?" Clint asked.

Without blinking an eye, Ahiga replied, "I burned it. His words mean nothing and a man like that cannot be trusted to uphold any bond."

As much as Clint would have liked something more concrete to wave in front of Farelli's face as some sort of bargaining chip, he couldn't deny that Ahiga had a valid point. "That letter was probably worth less than the paper it was written on, but it would have been nice to wave it under Farelli's nose. Apparently, just thinking that a letter from him could find its way to the Federals is enough to make him nervous, and that's just how we want him to be."

Clint rode through the clustered Indians until he was close enough to reach out and pull aside the blanket wrapped around the translator's head. "I'll take this," Clint said as he tore the markings from the skinny man's shoulder. "And this," he added as he peeled the spectacles from the translator's face.

"But . . . I need those," the translator whined as he eyed the spectacles.

"Considering you were present to help iron out deals that involved killing innocent folks on both sides of this bloodbath, I'd keep my mouth shut. This tribe's keeping you alive," Clint warned. "I'd say that's worth seeing badly for a little while."

The translator glanced about and nodded before wrapping the blanket back around his head.

Clint then rode over to Tolfox and asked, "What can you donate to the cause?"

FORTY-TWO

When Clint returned to Fort Winstead, he found the place in a state of celebration. It was no surprise that most of the raucous sounds and loud music were coming from the saloon. What did surprise Clint was that Colonel Farelli was in the middle of the merriment and raising his cup along with all the other soldiers.

Just as Clint was about to wade into the drunken mess, he was pulled aside by a strong grip that closed around his left wrist. After being turned around and nearly yanked from his feet, Clint felt a set of warm, eager lips press against his mouth. He recognized Abigail's kiss immediately.

"What was that for?" Clint asked once he was able to take a breath.

Abigail's face was dusty as ever and her hair was a wild tangle roughly tied behind her head. She smiled broadly and wrapped an arm around Clint's body while sliding one leg along his hip. "That was for letting me get so deep into the colonel's pockets that I won't have to work for a year. Why didn't you tell me you were gonna leave something more for them soldiers to find than just a bunch of empty old wagons?"

"What are you talking about?"

"We all heard the shooting," she said in a somewhat slurred whisper. "I was about to pretend to see somethin' else when those shots came and so I went to see if you needed help. I didn't find you, but I sure as hell found those dead Injuns you left behind." After thinking for a moment, she asked, "That was you, wasn't it?"

"Right, those were some of Tolfox's men," Clint told her.

"It didn't matter whose men they were," Abigail said. "The colonel was out to kill some Injuns, and finding those bodies made his day. The man's a damned vulture, but he promised a bonus for scalps and he paid up. You didn't get hurt or nothin', did you?"

Clint chuckled and replied, "No, but it's good to know that concern was so far down on your list."

"Aw, yer standin' here in front of me! It ain't like I thought a dead man could do that!"

Clint was about to ask if she was drunk, but a better question came to mind. "How drunk are you, Abigail?"

"Pretty damn drunk, but not too drunk to give you a hell of a ride."

"I think Farelli is trying to catch my attention, but don't you think for one second I'll forget about that offer you just made."

Abigail made a few more offers, but most of them were lost amid a chorus of whoops and hollers as another bottle of whiskey was opened and drinks were passed around. Now that he was in the saloon and among all the men, Clint noticed that only a few of the men were in Army uniforms. The rest looked like gunmen that could be found in any rowdy drinking hole.

Colonel Farelli had been waving to Clint on and off since Clint had walked into the place. Now the colonel was waving hard enough to throw his arm out of its socket. As much as he would have liked to see Farelli continue to flail and flap his wing like an idiot, Clint acknowledged the wave and walked over to Farelli's table.

"There he is!" Farelli shouted. "Just the man I wanted to see. Clint Adams! The Gunsmith himself!"

Nodding and standing beside Farelli, Clint patted the other man's shoulder and said, "No need to shout, Farelli. I'm right here."

"I owe you some money, Adams. We killed most of those murdering redskins and chased the rest of them into the hills. You did a hell of a job today!"

More than anything, Clint wanted to ask Farelli how he came up with such a colorful way to describe blowing up an empty camp and stumbling across some dead bodies.

"We even got us a prisoner!" Farelli continued. "He'll be swinging from a noose in the morning."

"Can I have a word with you?" Clint asked. "Maybe somewhere without all this noise?"

"If you want your money, I can pay you right here."

"It's not about any money. It's about some important business that needs to be handled."

"Then handle it with one of my clerks," Farelli said with a dismissive wave of his hand. "They know about my business matters."

"No," Clint told him, "this is going to be something you'll want to handle yourself."

FORTY-THREE

Clint waited outside of the saloon for a few minutes and watched drunken gunmen stagger in and out to collect their fees and free drinks. A few soldiers came and went as well, but most of them were busy doing their jobs instead of drinking with their commanding officer. When Farelli finally did make his appearance, it was amid a booming laugh and several halfhearted salutes from the hired guns.

"What is it, Adams?" Farelli asked as he walked over to where Clint was waiting. "I've got more celebrating to do."

Rather than say anything, Clint extended his hand to show the few items he was holding. Among them were the translator's spectacles and the black feathers that had hung from Tolfox's forearm. That sight seemed to cut through Farelli's whiskey haze real quickly.

"What are those?" Farelli demanded.

"Proof that your translator and Tolfox are still alive," Clint replied. "I thought you'd like to know about them so you'd know who'll be speaking against you at your court-martial."

"If I'm going to be brought up before anyone, it'll be to pin a few medals on me."

"Is that why you started this whole mess?" Clint asked. "To get some medals? I thought you'd just keep your head down and stay quiet since you got out of that business of stealing supplies and selling them for profit."

"I'm not the first one to ever be accused of that, you know."

"That's true, but I think most crooked officers draw the line at stirring up a whole bunch of angry Indians just so he can ride in to make the whole mess go away. You probably only hear about these attacks from what your men tell you or what you read in the newspapers, but real folks have been dying. Most of those folks had been just going about their lives when they were pulled into this little Indian war you started."

Farelli grabbed hold of Clint's arm so he could drag him away from the saloon. Although Clint went along with him for a few steps, he easily pulled out of the other man's grasp. When Farelli spoke again, his drunken bluster was gone and his voice was reduced to a harsh whisper. "Those redskins have always been attacking wagons and settlers. And in case you haven't noticed, most of the men getting hurt of late have been my soldiers!"

"And why is that, Colonel?" Clint asked, mentioning Farelli's rank as if it were a slur. "Could it be that your men were put into danger when they should have been dispatched somewhere they were truly needed? Or were they always in your pocket like these killers you hired to chase the old folks and women from their camp?"

"Those attacks were real."

"They were set up!" Clint shot back. "I've spoken to the man who carried them out. I've spoken to the man who was at every meeting between you and Tolfox. I know you were working with Tolfox back when he was named Proud Fox, and don't even try to act like you don't know that name because you mentioned it earlier, yourself!"

Retracting a bit when he heard the fire in Clint's voice, Farelli said, "I could have you booted out of here for talking to me like that. Some might even consider this grounds for—"

"Grounds for what?" Clint interrupted. "Lying? Stealing? Killing? I know one of us is guilty of those things, and it's not me. You know damn well what you did and so did these two," he said as he tightened his fist around the items in his hand and held them up for Farelli to see.

Farelli slapped away Clint's hand and snarled, "These trinkets don't mean shit!"

"Maybe not, but both the men they belong to can put an end to this bloody scam you've been running. Tolfox knows you've been gunning for him. First you sent Nolan, who killed some of the few truly good soldiers under your command, and then you charged into that camp tossing sticks of dynamite."

"That translator's a whiny piece of milquetoast," Farelli said. "He wouldn't dare stand against me."

"He would if he thought that display at that camp was meant for him. And, come to think of it, someone may just have given him that idea."

Farelli slowly shook his head. "Fine. It's all over. I've used up all my favors and I won't try to collect any more. Wherever Tolfox is, he can stay there. We're done. You happy?"

Clint shook his head. "Too late for that. Too much blood was spilled and someone's got to answer for it. Tolfox will be paying up, and you can't just sit here in your own little fort, no matter how pathetic it is."

"So what do you want from me, Adams?"

"You're a disgrace to your uniform. I want you to stand trial for what you've done so the Army can know who managed to somehow slither this far up through the ranks. We're going to gather up whatever you need to take with you and then I'm escorting you out of here so we can go to a proper Army officer and set this matter straight. After all this scrambling around and scurrying in the shadows, it should be a relief to be done with it once and for all."

There was plenty of fire in Farelli's eyes as he glanced

back and forth. A few soldiers looked toward him and Clint, but they ignored whatever was going on and kept walking, just as they had for all the other times when the colonel had conducted his business in the shadows. "I don't suppose you'd allow me to wrap things up my own way?"

"No," Clint replied. "I wouldn't. I tried to let the cards fall where they may the last time I caught you with your hand in the till. This time, I'm doing everything I can to put you where you'll need a miracle to slither out of it again."

Farelli's jaw clenched and his lips twitched as if he was silently listing all of his possible escape routes. Once he reached the end of that short list, he let out the breath he'd been holding and said, "I've got documents I'll need for my defense. Will you let me go to my office to fetch them?"

"I'll go along with you," Clint said. "But if you step out of line, I've got more than enough to justify burying you in the middle of this place."

FORTY-FOUR

Colonel Farelli was a beaten man. Clint could tell that much in the way Farelli walked and the way he hung his head. Every last one of Farelli's steps was the heavy, shuffling movement of someone walking to the end of his trail.

Even so, Clint kept his hand close to his gun and his eyes open for any sign of treachery. Farelli may have been a pathetic, cowardly excuse for a soldier, but he hadn't survived this long by being stupid. Once desperation was added to the mix, the colonel became a genuine threat to Clint's well-being.

While inside his shack, Farelli sifted through a couple drawers and pulled together a collection of documents that looked mostly like a bunch of letters. There were a few papers bearing the Army seal upon them, but Clint wasn't about to study each and every one. Farelli was guilty. There were already witnesses to testify to that and there would surely be more stepping forward. If need be, Clint intended on gathering those witnesses himself. He didn't expect it would be too difficult to convince the lesser rats to save their own skins by sacrificing their leader.

"All right," Clint said. "That's enough. Let's go."

Farelli looked at him with the expression of a lost child.

His eyes were wide and his mouth hung open. "Oh . . . all right. Can I ride my own horse?"

Now, Clint couldn't help but find the situation pathetic. At any moment, he expected Farelli to make an even bigger mockery of himself and the uniform he wore. "We'll take whatever horse we can find. Let's just go." Placing his hand upon his gun, Clint added, "Right now."

Nodding weakly, Farelli clutched his papers to his chest and walked out of the shack. Rather than turn toward the stable, he looked over at the saloon.

"No, Farelli. This way."

But Farelli didn't even glance at Clint. He still had his papers pressed against himself when he barked, "A thousand dollars to whoever kills this man!"

Clint grabbed Farelli's arm and dragged him toward the stable.

"He's kidnapping me!" Farelli cried. "A thousand to whoever guns the bastard down!"

At first, none of the men standing outside of the saloon took much notice. But when a few of them were able to see Farelli's face as well as Clint dragging him away, they walked toward the shack.

"That you, Colonel?" one of the gunmen asked.

"Yes, it's me! Kill this man!"

That was all it took to light a fire under the gunmen. They had come to Fort Winstead to fight and most of them were drunk. It wasn't a good combination.

"Oh, hell," Clint said as the first gunman drew his pistol.

The first few rounds were wild and hissed through the air around Clint and Farelli. Clint drew the modified Colt and jumped back a few steps so he could put the shack between himself and the saloon. More bullets flew, shattering windows and punching through the flimsy wooden planks. As more gunmen joined the fray, the bullets moved closer to their target.

Clint swore under his breath when he realized Farelli

had ducked back into the shack. Once inside, the colonel could arm himself or even slip out another door, and Clint had gone through too much to let Farelli escape now.

Circling around the shack, Clint discovered there wasn't a back door and there were no other windows. He stepped around to the front, preparing himself for the worst, and that was exactly what he got. At least eight gunmen were walking toward the shack. Each man had a gun in his hand and all of their faces lit up when they caught sight of Clint.

"There he is!" one of them shouted.

Two of the gunmen swung their aim toward Clint and pulled their triggers. Even as bullets drilled through the shack on one side of him and hissed through the air on the other, Clint waited until he knew he had no other choice before squeezing his trigger. The Colt barked twice in quick succession, knocking both of the gunmen from their feet. Clint waited a few more seconds before firing again.

Just as Clint had hoped, a few of the gunmen scattered when they saw a couple of their own hit the dirt. Some froze and the rest forged ahead with guns blazing. Clint ducked around the shack, waited a few seconds, and then looked around the corner again. This time, Clint dropped to one knee so his head emerged at a much lower point than it had before. That little trick bought him the fraction of a second he needed to fire a few more rounds.

One of Clint's bullets ripped through a gunman's knee, sending the man to the ground where he could curl up into a writhing bundle. Another bullet punched into a gunman's hip, spinning him around like a top while the man fired wildly into the air. Clint's third shot didn't find its mark, but got close enough to send a man running for cover. Knowing that he only had one more bullet in his cylinder, Clint fired it over the gunmen's heads before pulling himself back around the shack so he could reload.

As his fingers flew through the motions of pulling out the empty casings and replacing them with fresh ones from his gun belt, Clint pressed his ear against the shack. The wall was just thin enough for him to hear Farelli stomping around inside. Even though Clint could hear plenty of shouted cursing within the shack, he was more concerned by the shattering of glass and the low roar of a fire bursting to life.

Clint ran around to the front of the cabin as more gunmen ventured closer to the rickety little building. Raising his gun and turning to see if he needed to shoot, Clint found one of the gunmen taking aim at him with a rifle. Before Clint could pull his trigger, a shot was fired from somewhere else and the rifleman keeled over.

"Who's next?" Abigail hollered as she pointed her smoking gun at the largest group of hired shooters.

While some of the gunmen seemed ready to accept her challenge, most of them were put off by the fact that they'd have to fight a woman to do so. Apparently, the rifleman didn't have any friends among the killers, because none of them stepped up to avenge him.

Kicking open the shack's door, Clint found Farelli standing inside amid a growing fire. The flames spread outward from his desk, lapping at the walls and quickly moving along the dry wood.

"The Indians did this!" Farelli shouted. "That's what they'll think! Nobody will ever know what happened here! Any Federals coming around will think those redskins burned this place down and that you helped them!"

There was no mistaking the crazy fire in Farelli's eyes. It burned brighter than the flames that were consuming the cabin.

Farelli's chest heaved as he looked around at the flames closing in around him. "I hear them now. Don't you hear the Indians, Adams? They're coming, just like I said. Just you watch!"

"Get the hell out of here before you're cooked alive!" Clint shouted. "You'll set this whole damn place on fire!"

But Farelli was beyond talking now. The moment he felt the fire on his sleeve, he started to twitch and flail his arm. His motion only added to the flames and soon his whole upper body was engulfed in them. Farelli let out a wild cry and ran at Clint like some sort of demon loosed from the pits of hell.

Clint thought Farelli might have tried something stupid to get himself out of the mess he'd made, but this went well beyond Clint's expectations. The more Farelli moved, the more the fire blazed around him. When he saw Farelli charge at him, Clint's first instinct was just to hop out of the way.

Farelli bolted past Clint, ran out of the shack, and immediately started running toward the nearby stable. In that instant, Clint could imagine the stable burning down with all those horses inside of it. Soon, the entire fort would be one giant fireball.

When Clint fired his next shot, it was to prevent Farelli from making an already bad situation even worse. After the colonel dropped and flailed on the ground, Clint fired another round into him as an act of mercy.

"Where's the fire brigade?" Clint shouted to the closest soldier that had come rushing at the sound of all the shooting.

The soldier simply looked stunned. "Fire brigade?"

"A bucket line! Just some damn water to put out these flames! What the hell do you do in case of a fire?"

"I don't . . . we don't . . . we never . . ."

Clint shook his head and walked away from the shack. Suddenly, he started to wonder if Farelli's madness had infected him as well. He could hear the Indians. Looking toward the front gate, Clint realized the sound was real. There were Indians outside and they were rushing into the fort with weapons drawn. The first face Clint picked out was Ahiga's. Then he spotted Elsu and plenty of other Navajo braves.

The gunmen that had come out to claim Farelli's thousand dollars fired a few shots at the Indians, but quickly decided to cut and run. Most of the soldiers went to the bunkhouse and stable to collect their horses and possessions before scattering from the burning fort along with the civilians who worked there. The only ones who weren't abandoning Fort Winstead were the Navajo warriors, Clint, and Abigail.

"What in the hell went wrong?" Abigail asked.

"Just about everything." Clint sighed. Seeing Ahiga walk toward him, Clint gave the Navajo a tired wave. "What brings you folks here?" he asked.

"You helped us clean up our tribe," Ahiga replied. "So Chief Mingan thought we could help you clean out yours."

"You still got that translator?"

Ahiga nodded.

"Let him go. He may be better off with your people than out here, so remember he was just doing a simple job and could use your help. If he doesn't want it, just let him be."

"And Tolfox?" Ahiga asked.

Clint walked to the hitching post where Eclipse was tied and loosened the reins. The horses were already gone from the stable and everyone from cooks to soldiers were riding away. Already the fort felt empty as the crackle of flames became steadily louder. When he caught sight of Fawn among the Indians just outside the gate, Clint gave her a weary smile.

"Tolfox dragged your people into this whole mess," Clint said. "You should be the ones to deal with him. I trust you won't be attacking any more wagon trains from now on."

The big Navajo raised his nose and pulled in a deep breath of smoky air. "I am He Who Fights. If there is another war, I will fight."

Clint was too tired to argue. Shots had been fired and blood had been spilled on both sides of this fight. With Tolfox, Farelli, and all of the killers who blindly followed them out of the picture, this fight was over. "Just try not fighting for a while, huh?" Clint requested. "You may just like it."

"And what of this place?" Ahiga asked as he looked around at the burning fort.

"This place should bum to the ground," Clint replied. "That's all a straw man's good for anyway."

Watch for

THE GREATER EVIL

321st novel in the exciting GUNSMITH series
from Jove

Coming in September!

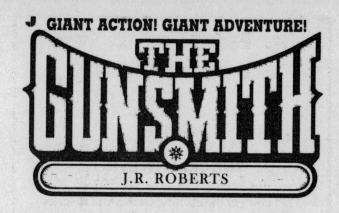

GIANT ACTION! GIANT ADVENTURE!

THE GUNSMITH

J.R. ROBERTS

Little Sureshot And
The Wild West Show
(Gunsmith Giant #9)

Dead Weight
(Gunsmith Giant #10)

Red Mountain
(Gunsmith Giant #11)

The Knights of Misery
(Gunsmith Giant #12)

penguin.com

M228AS1207